Adapted from the originals by Anne McKie, illustrated by Ken McKie.

This edition published 1994

Published by
Grandreams Limited
Jadwin House, 205/211 Kentish Town Road, London, NW5 2JU.

Printed in Czech Republic

ISBN 0 86227 869 4

LO2

# My Biggest Book of
# Favourite
# Tales

**This book belongs to**

.....................................

.....................................

.....................................

**Age** ...........................

**Favourite tales in this book**

# GULLIVER'S TRAVELS

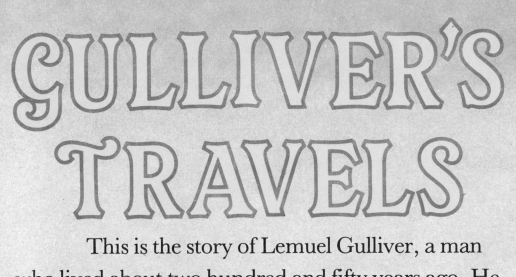

This is the story of Lemuel Gulliver, a man who lived about two hundred and fifty years ago. He studied very hard and after many years, he became a doctor. He longed to travel and loved the sea, so he became a doctor on board a sailing ship.

One day he set off on a long voyage to the South Seas on a ship called the Antelope — and here begins one of the strangest adventure stories ever told.

All went well on the Antelope for the first few weeks. Then suddenly one night, a great storm sprang up, the ship hit a rock and was wrecked.

Although the sea was rough and the waves high, Gulliver was such a strong swimmer that he managed to reach the shore. Completely exhausted, he dragged himself up the beach as far away from the sea as possible. He lay down on the first grassy bank he found and fell into a deep sleep.

At daybreak, when he opened his eyes, he tried to sit up and look around — but he was tied to the ground! He couldn't move his arms or legs or even lift his head.

Then Gulliver felt something alive running up his legs and across his chest — like a crowd of mice or several beetles perhaps!

All at once, Gulliver let out a great roar of surprise. For standing on his chest were at least forty men, each about six inches high. Gulliver's great roar startled the little men. Quickly they slid down to the floor below, where great crowds of tiny people were assembled.

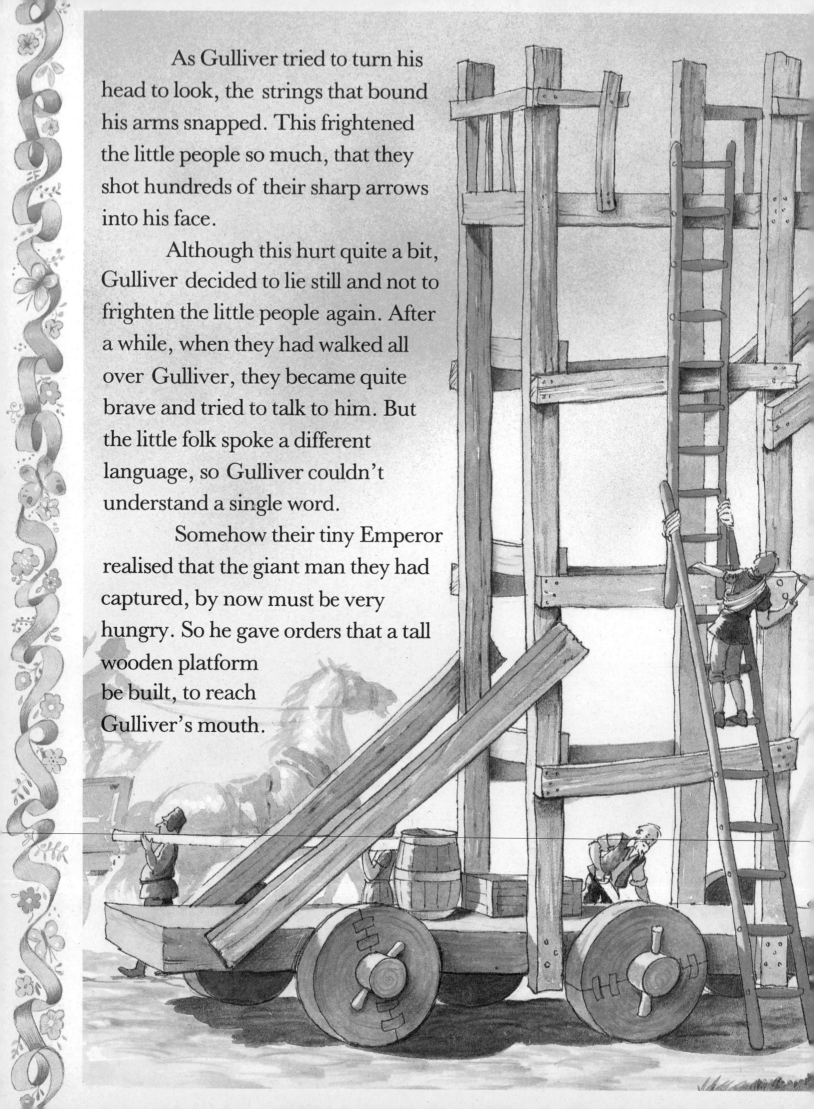

As Gulliver tried to turn his head to look, the strings that bound his arms snapped. This frightened the little people so much, that they shot hundreds of their sharp arrows into his face.

Although this hurt quite a bit, Gulliver decided to lie still and not to frighten the little people again. After a while, when they had walked all over Gulliver, they became quite brave and tried to talk to him. But the little folk spoke a different language, so Gulliver couldn't understand a single word.

Somehow their tiny Emperor realised that the giant man they had captured, by now must be very hungry. So he gave orders that a tall wooden platform be built, to reach Gulliver's mouth.

After a while, several cartloads of food and wine arrived. And hundreds of the tiny men climbed up the platform with baskets of bread and meat. The hungry Gulliver drank a whole barrel of their wine in one gulp, and ate a basket full of loaves in one bite.

The Lilliputians (for that is what the little people were called) kept bringing more and more until Gulliver was so full up, he fell fast asleep.

The little people seemed to have lost all fear of the gigantic Gulliver, so while he slept, thousands of them set to work. Five hundred carpenters made a platform on wheels, and nine hundred men hoisted the sleeping Gulliver onto it. Then with five hundred guards either side and one thousand five hundred horses pulling hard, they began to move him towards their capital city.

It took a whole day and night to reach their destination. At last the procession came to a halt outside a large church, which was to be Gulliver's house — although it seemed as small as a dog kennel to him.

The tiny Emperor of Lilliput did not intend setting Gulliver free altogether. He ordered all his blacksmiths to make a thick chain and padlock it onto Gulliver's leg, so he could move around — but not very far.

News soon spread of the giant the Emperor had captured. People flocked in from all over the land of Lilliput, until the city was jammed with the little folk.

Six hundred of them were chosen to look after Gulliver, and four hundred tailors were kept busy making him new clothes. Six of Lilliput's finest scholars were sent to teach him their language.

At last the Emperor could understand Gulliver when he asked to be set free. He finally agreed, on one condition. Gulliver must empty his pockets of anything that could be dangerous to Lilliput.

Out came a knife, a comb and a razor. The little people were fascinated. Then came his handkerchief — which to them looked like a carpet. His snuffbox seemed like a huge chest full of gunpowder; his watch made more noise than a water-mill, and they thought that his purse was a fishing net.

Finally Gulliver took out his pistol and fired it into the air. So great was the noise, thousands of the little people fell flat on their backs with shock. Only the Emperor stood his ground. For a man only six inches high, he was very brave.

But even the brave Emperor feared
something. And one day he came to ask Gulliver's help.

On the island of nearby Blefuscu lived a people
called the Big-Endians. Their fleet of fifty ships had
just set sail to invade Lilliput.

What a shock the poor Big-Endian sailors got
when Gulliver waded out to sea, roped all their ships
together, and dragged them back to Lilliput.

It didn't take Gulliver very long to realise that
the Emperor of Lilliput was only using him to fight his
battles for him, and that the Big-Endians were not a
wicked people at all. So Gulliver made his mind up to
go over to their island and live with them.

He took a large warship from Lilliput, loaded it up with his clothes (so they wouldn't get wet), then towed it behind him to their island of Blefuscu.

He was most kindly received by the little folk, but all Gulliver really wanted was to get back to England.

Quite by chance as Gulliver was walking on top of the cliff, he saw something floating in the sea. He could hardly believe his eyes — it was a full size rowing boat floating upside down.

Straight away the Emperor of the Big-Endians sent every ship in his fleet out to sea to tow it back to shore.

It took two thousand men to turn the boat right side up and then begin to repair it. Five hundred people stitched day and night to make the sails. Everyone on the island worked hard until the boat was ready.

Gulliver took on board several tiny live sheep and cows to take back home. Then sadly came the time to say farewell.

After only two days at sea, Gulliver was picked up by a sailing ship heading for England. When he told his strange story, the captain could hardly believe it — until he saw the tiny cows and sheep which Gulliver placed on the table in front of him.

At last Gulliver returned home. People were delighted to welcome him back, and never tired of hearing his strange story.

# THE FROG PRINCE

Once upon a time there lived a King who had several beautiful daughters, but the youngest was even more beautiful than the rest.

Near the castle of this King was a large and gloomy forest. Just a short walk into the trees was a small clearing. At the far side stood an old lime tree, and beneath its branches splashed a fountain in the middle of a dark deep pool.

Whenever it was very hot, the King's youngest daughter would run off into this wood and sit by the pool, throwing her golden ball into the air. This was her favorite pastime.

One afternoon when the Princess threw the ball high up in the air — she didn't catch it! It slipped through her fingers onto the grass. Then it rolled past her into the fountain, and disappeared beneath the water.

The Princess peered into the pool, but her precious golden ball was gone. Quickly, she plunged her arms into the pool as far as she could reach, but she could feel nothing except weeds and water lilies. Some people said the pool was so deep — it had no bottom. So when the Princess realised her golden ball was gone for ever, she began to cry. ''Come back to me this minute, golden ball,'' sobbed the Princess, staring hard into the water.

Now as a rule, Princesses are used to getting their own way. So after her golden ball didn't magically pop up out of the water, she started to howl even louder. Dear, oh dear! First she stamped her feet and then she threw herself down on the grass in temper.

The Princess was making so much noise, that she didn't notice a big green frog stick his head out of the water and jump onto the grass beside her. ''Don't cry, beautiful Princess,'' the frog croaked. ''I saw your golden ball fall into the water, and it will be my pleasure to dive down and get it for you — if you will give me something in return.''

At this the Princess cheered up. "I will gladly give you my jewels and pearls, even my golden crown, if you will bring back my golden ball." It's true to say that promises should never be made in a hurry, even by Princesses, because a promise is a thing that must be kept — especially to frogs!

The frog hopped nearer to the Princess. "Pearls and jewels and golden crowns are no use to me," he went on, "but if you'll love me and be my friend, if you'll let me eat from your golden plate, drink from your golden cup, and sleep on your golden bed, I will dive down and fetch your ball."

So eager was the Princess to see her golden ball once more, that she didn't listen too carefully to what the frog had to say. "I promise you all you ask, if only you will bring back my ball."

Quick as a flash, the frog jumped into the pool then bobbed up again with the ball in his mouth. Straight away the King's daughter snatched her ball and ran back to the castle.

"Take me with you," cried the frog. "I cannot run as fast as you and I shall be left behind."

But the Princess didn't care about her promise and soon forgot all about the frog. Later that day, when the Princess was sitting at the table, something was heard coming up the marble stairs, "Splish, splosh." The sound came nearer and nearer and a voice cried, "Let me in, youngest daughter of the King."

The Princess jumped up to see who had called her. Now when she caught sight of the frog, she turned very pale.

"What does a frog want with you?" demanded the King, looking rather surprised.

The Princess hung her head. "When I was sitting playing by the fountain my golden ball fell into the water. This frog fetched it back for me — because I cried so much." The Princess started to cry again. "I promised to love him and let him eat from my golden plate, drink from my golden cup, and sleep on my golden bed."

The King looked at the frog and thought for a while before he spoke. "Then you must keep your promise, my daughter."

The Princess knew she must obey, so she beckoned the frog to come inside. The frog hopped in after her and jumped up into her chair and straight onto the table. "Now push your golden plate near me," said the frog, "so that we may eat together." As she did so, the frog leapt onto her plate and gobbled up all her dinner, which was just as well, because the Princess didn't feel much like eating.

Next, the frog drank from her little golden cup until it was quite empty. Somehow the Princess didn't feel at all thirsty either! After the frog had finished, he took one great leap and landed on the Princess's knee. "Go away you ugly cold frog!" she screamed. "I will never let you sleep on my lovely clean bed!"

This made the King very angry. "This frog helped you when you needed it. Now you must keep your promise to him."

"I am very tired after that wonderful meal," the frog said, "and you did promise that I could go to sleep on your golden bed."

Very unwillingly the Princess picked up the frog and carried him upstairs to her room.

When the frog hopped into the middle of her golden bed, it was just too much for the Princess. She tugged hard at the coverlet and tipped the poor frog onto the floor.

As he fell he was changed into a handsome Prince. A spell had been cast on him by an evil witch and only the Princess had the power to break it.

The Princess was speechless. She felt very sorry indeed that she had been so unkind to the frog.

After a while, the handsome Prince and the Princess got married, and I'm sure lived happily ever after.

# CINDERELLA

Once upon a time, there lived a Baron whose wife died, leaving him to bring up their little girl.

A few years later, when his daughter had grown into a beautiful young lady, the Baron married again. But sadly, soon after, he became ill and died.

His second wife was mean and cruel with a very nasty temper. And to make matters worse, she had two daughters of her own who were even worse than she was. One was very fat, one was very thin and both of them were extremely ugly. In fact, people called them the Ugly Sisters — behind their backs of course!

After the Baron's death, his daughter was treated like a servant by the stepmother and her two ugly girls. They forced her to do all the rough work in the house. The poor girl toiled from dawn to dusk, scrubbing floors and washing greasy pots and pans.

The hardest job of all was cleaning out the many fire-grates in the castle. The cinders and soot marked the girl's dress, her hands got grubby and there were black smudges on her nose. That is why the Ugly Sisters unkindly nicknamed her Cinderella.

At night, when all her work was done, Cinderella would sit by the kitchen fire warming her toes near the cinders before she went upstairs to her cold attic room.

One day at the Royal Palace the King's son announced that he was to give a splendid Ball. To their great joy Cinderella's two step-sisters received an invitation. "You must make us both new ball gowns at once!" one sister yelled at Cinderella. "And do our hair to make us look more beautiful," screeched the other.

This meant that Cinderella had even more work to do. All day long she stitched and sewed. Every pleat, every frill and every bit of lace had to be just right. Not to mention the extra washing, starching and ironing of all their frilly petticoats.

In spite of all the lovely clothes Cinderella had made them, the two sisters still looked dreadfully ugly.

At last the coach arrived to take the Ugly Sisters to the ball. Not one word of thanks did Cinderella get! The nasty pair pushed and shoved their way into their seats, and drove off with their noses in the air.

Sadly, Cinderella went back into the kitchen to sit by the fire. All of a sudden, a log on the fire burst into flames filling the kitchen with light. In the brightness Cinderella noticed, for the first time, a little old lady in a cloak and pointed hat — standing right next to her.

"I am your Fairy Godmother," she said kindly, "and you are going to the Ball!"

Cinderella was too surprised to speak. She had no idea she had a Fairy Godmother.

"Now quickly," the fairy said, "go into the garden and fetch me a pumpkin." Next, she told Cinderella to bring her the six mice and three rats that were caught in the trap near the kitchen cupboard. And last of all, she asked for six lizards from behind the garden shed.

With one wave of her wand the pumpkin was transformed into a glittering golden coach. The six mice turned into fine grey horses. The three rats became handsome coachmen, and lo and behold, the six lizards were smart footmen.

"Well, Cinderella, now you are ready to go to the ball," said her Godmother. "Oh dear, I almost forgot your dress!"

Once more she waved her wand and Cinderella's ragged clothes were changed into a magnificent silver dress which sparkled with precious stones, and there on Cinderella's feet were a pair of glistening glass slippers, which fitted perfectly.

As she was about to drive off in her golden coach, her Godmother called after her, "You must leave the ball before the clock strikes midnight — for my magic only lasts until then." And with a last wave of her wand she vanished.

Cinderella's coach was the last to arrive at the Palace. All the guests in the ballroom turned to look at Cinderella as the Prince stepped forward to greet her.

She danced so well and looked so beautiful that the Prince fell in love with her straight away.

Everyone that night was whispering about the lovely stranger who had captured the heart of the Prince. And Cinderella was so happy she lost all count of time.

All of a sudden the Palace clock struck
midnight. Cinderella dashed from the ballroom as fast
as she could. Halfway down the grand staircase she
lost one of her glass slippers.

As she ran through the Palace gardens her
wonderful ballgown turned back into rags.

No golden coach was waiting outside to take
her home, instead, lying there on the ground was a
pumpkin, and running away were all the mice, the
rats and the six lizards.

Cinderella ran back home through the night,
and hid in the dark corner of the kitchen. But when
she felt in her apron pocket — she found one sparkling
glass slipper.

Meanwhile, as the Prince rushed through his Palace searching for her, he found the other slipper on the stairs and picked it up. Desperately the Prince asked every guest at the Ball, and all his servants, but no-one knew the name of the lovely girl.

The very next morning the glass slipper was placed on a velvet cushion and taken to the city square. ''I shall marry the girl whose foot fits this glass slipper,'' announced the Prince.

What excitement this caused! Every girl in the kingdom wanted to try on the slipper. Princesses, serving maids, rich girls, poor girls, all tried — but it was far too small for any of them.

When it came to the Ugly Sisters' turns, they fought and squabbled who should try it on first. They tried their hardest to squeeze their great clumsy feet into the dainty slipper — but it was no use.

All this time Cinderella had been sitting very quietly in the corner. Luckily, the Prince's servant noticed her. He placed the glass slipper on the velvet cushion in front of her. Gently she slipped it on her tiny foot — and it fitted perfectly. Then she took the other slipper from her apron pocket and, of course, they matched.

The Prince was overjoyed to find his lost love and begged Cinderella to be his bride.

The wedding was a splendid affair, with the Fairy Godmother as chief guest. The Ugly Sisters promised to mend their ways — and everyone lived happily ever after.

# ALI BABA

Long ago in an eastern land, there lived two brothers, Cassim and Ali Baba. The elder brother Cassim married a very rich wife and didn't have to work at all.

Ali Baba, on the other hand, married a girl as poor as himself, and he had to work very hard for a living. Every day he went to the forest to look for firewood. Then he would load up his donkeys and try to sell his wood in the market place.

One morning while Ali Baba was in the forest chopping wood, he heard the sound of many horses approaching. Now Ali Baba knew there were bands of fierce robbers that roamed the forest — so quickly as possible, he climbed up the nearest tree for safety. Instead of thundering by, as Ali Baba expected, all forty robbers came to a sudden halt. Quickly they dismounted and tethered their horses next to the very spot where Ali Baba was hiding.

The leader of the robbers strode up to a nearby rock and said in a loud voice, "Open sesame!" At these words a door in the rock swung open leading to a cave beyond. One by one the forty thieves disappeared inside, carrying with them huge sacks of silver and gold they had unloaded from their horses. The door slammed shut after the last robber had stepped inside. Poor Ali Baba dared not climb down from his hiding place for fear of his life.

After what seemed a very long uncomfortable
wait, the forty thieves came out of the cave empty-
handed. The robber chief raised his arms and cried,
"Close sesame!" and the door in the rock shut tight.
The robbers jumped back on their horses and rode
away.

Plucking up all his courage, Ali Baba jumped
down from the tree and ran over to the rock. "Open
sesame!" he cried in a trembling voice. Straight away,
the door swung open and Ali Baba found himself in a
gigantic cave.

What wonders met his eyes! Sacks full of silver and gold, priceless carpets, ornaments of ivory and jade and endless chests of precious jewels. Hurriedly, Ali Baba grabbed a couple of the bags of gold, ran out of the cave, and loaded up his donkeys.

When Ali Baba's wife saw all that gold, she was overjoyed. "It is far too much to count," she whispered quite breathless. "We must measure it into small sacks and hide it, for if we spend it a little at a time, no-one will suspect we have the robbers' gold."

So off she ran to the elder brother, Cassim's house to borrow a measure. This made Cassim's wife very suspicious. ''Ali Baba's wife is far too poor to need a measure,'' she thought to herself. So secretly she stuck a small piece of wax to the bottom — so that whatever was put in the measure would stick.

Sure enough when the measure was returned next day, one shiny gold coin was stuck to the wax. It really puzzled Cassim and his wife.

The following morning, Ali Baba set out as usual for the forest. But this time his brother Cassim was following him secretly. As soon as Ali Baba reached the rock, he uttered the magic words, ''Open sesame!'' the door opened and he stepped inside. Very soon he reappeared loaded down with gold and jewels.

The greedy Cassim couldn't wait to try. As soon as Ali Baba was out of sight, Cassim stood in front of the rock, "Open sesame," he shouted, and the door opened at once. Cassim wasted no time, he rushed into the cave and began filling sacks of gold himself. But alas, when the time came for him to open the door — he had forgotten the magic words. He tried everything but the door remained shut tight!

Later that day the robbers returned. They were such evil and cruel men, that in their anger they killed Cassim and cut him up into four pieces!

Late that night when Cassim didn't return, his wife told Ali Baba how Cassim had followed him into the forest to spy on him. Ali Baba guessed what had happened. In the middle of the night he returned to the robbers' cave and found his poor dead brother just inside the entrance.

He loaded the four pieces of the body onto his donkey and returned home to break the terrible news to Cassim's wife. After much weeping, the family decided that Cassim's body must be sewn together before he could be buried (that way no-one would know he had been cut into pieces by the thieves).

A faithful family slave called Morgiana knew
of an old blind cobbler who could do the task. In the
dead of night she led the old man to Cassim's house.
Skilfully he stitched the four pieces together, so no-one
would know that Cassim had not died in his sleep. As
soon as he had finished, Morgiana led him back home
through the dark city streets.

Meanwhile, the forty thieves returned to their
cave. When they found that Cassim's body had
vanished they realised someone else knew of their
hiding place. They rode into the city and began to
question everyone. It wasn't long before the blind
cobbler told them of his unusual task the night before.

Although he was blind, he could easily remember the path that led to Cassim's house. The leader of the thieves marked the door with a large cross — so his men could return later and kill everyone inside. But clever Morgiana came along and marked every door in the street with a cross to confuse the thieves — and their evil plan was foiled.

All too soon, the robber chief heard about Ali Baba, who had once been a poor woodcutter, and was now the richest man in the city. It didn't take him long to guess it was Ali Baba who knew the secret of their cave.

So, the leader of the robbers disguised himself as a merchant selling oil. He called at Ali Baba's house asking for a night's lodging. With him he had a team of donkeys, each one loaded with a great jar. In every jar was hiding one of his evil band. Only one of the jars contained oil. That night when the household was fast asleep, the thieves planned to jump out and kill everyone.

Quite by chance, Morgiana ran out of oil for cooking. "I will borrow a little from the Merchant's jar," she thought to herself.

It was then she discovered the thieves' trick. The cunning girl filled a huge pan full of oil from the jar and heated it up on the stove. When it was boiling hot she tipped some into every jar — and the forty thieves were scalded to death.

While all this was going on, Ali Baba was
entertaining the robber chief, whom he had not
recognised. When Ali Baba asked Morgiana to dance
for his guest, she gladly agreed. As she danced she
leapt forward and plunged a dagger into the robber
chief's heart. It was only then that Ali Baba realised
how he had been tricked, and how brave Morgiana
was.

This story has a happy ending, for Morgiana
was given her freedom and married Ali Baba's son.
And everyone lived happily to the end of their days.

# THE EMPEROR'S NEW CLOTHES

A very long time ago, there lived an Emperor who loved new clothes. He wasn't a bit like other Emperors, who spent their days ruling their people or inspecting their soldiers. This Emperor was different! His days were spent trying on fancy new clothes, and admiring himself in one hundred full length mirrors!

Every bedroom in his enormous Palace was filled from floor to ceiling with wardrobes. Every wardrobe was so packed with clothes — not even the tiniest silk handkerchief would fit inside. Upstairs in the Palace was bad enough, but downstairs was even worse.

All the rooms and even the corridors were full of people waiting to see the Emperor. There were tailors, weavers, shoe-makers, dressmakers. Merchants with rolls of velvet and satin. Shopkeepers selling fancy shirts with frilly collars. Not to mention the jewellers! Out of their cases tumbled silver buckles, jewelled belts, sparkling rings and golden chains, each one costing a fortune.

The Emperor couldn't resist anything. He bought the lot. And to make matters worse, he told them all to come back the next day to show him more.

One day, two strangers arrived at the Emperor's Palace, pretending to be weavers, "We must see the Emperor at once," shouted the two rogues all the time trying not to laugh. For they had thought of a very clever plan which could make them very rich indeed. "We must see the Emperor in secret," cried the two rogues, as they strode through the Palace together.

"Clear the room and lock all the doors," the Emperor commanded as the two weavers bowed low in front of him. Excitedly they told the Emperor that they had discovered the secret of weaving magic cloth.

The Emperor looked spellbound. Then the weavers went on to explain, "To a wise and clever man like Your Majesty, the cloth is the finest ever seen — but to a fool it is completely invisible."

The Emperor could hardly believe his ears. He begged the weavers to start work straight away. "Bring your loom to the Palace this very day, and I will give you a bag of gold," the Emperor cried. "I must have a suit made from this magic cloth, then at last I shall be able to find out those around me that are fools."

Later that day the two weavers set up their loom in a room at the Palace. They pretended to work very hard, but of course, the loom was empty. Day after day the rogues spent long hours in front of their loom — doing nothing at all! And every day they asked the Emperor for another bag of gold for payment.

Weeks passed, until the Emperor could wait no longer. "If I go myself, and I cannot see the cloth, the weavers will know I am a fool," thought the Emperor. "But if I send my Prime Minister, then I shall find out for sure if he is a fool."

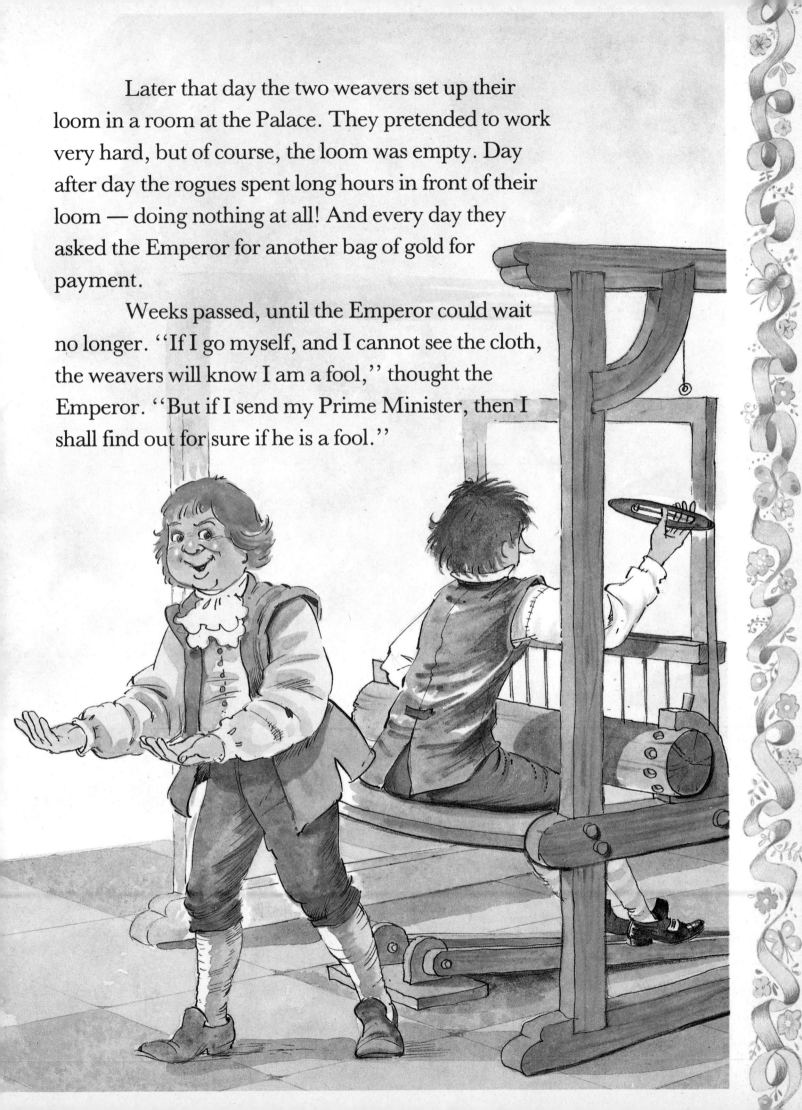

Now, the Prime Minister was rather old and short-sighted. Try as he may, he could not see even one piece of thread on the loom. ''I must be a complete fool,'' he muttered to himself. However, not wishing to lose his job he scurried off to tell the Emperor what he had found. ''Magnificent, exquisite, the finest piece of cloth ever woven,'' he puffed, quite out of breath.

The Emperor pushed him aside. "I simply must see for myself." He ran through the Palace and burst into the weavers' workroom, and all the people in his court followed him.

When the Emperor saw the empty loom he gasped, and so did everybody else. Not one of them could see a thing! As no-one wished to look a fool, they all waited for the Emperor to speak first.

He walked slowly round and round the loom thinking to himself, "I can't see a thing. I must be a fool and not fit to be Emperor."

So, he took a deep breath and faced his whole court. "It's exquisite, magnificent, quite wonderful!" he exclaimed. And everyone present, not wishing to appear foolish, congratulated the clever weavers.

"I must have the finest suit made to wear at tomorrow's parade," announced the Emperor. Then he gave the two weavers several more bags of gold, to work all night to finish the invisible suit.

The weavers could hardly believe their good fortune that the Emperor could be such a fool! The clever rogues measured the Emperor and then pretended to cut and sew the invisible cloth. At first light next morning they rushed into the Emperor's bedroom crying, "The wonderful magic suit is finished!"

The Emperor leapt out of bed, and the crafty pair pretended to help him dress in the invisible coat and breeches.

"Splendid! Absolute perfection!" the weavers exclaimed, as they stepped back to admire the Emperor.

Soon the whole court crowded round to see. But as none of them wished to appear fools, they all agreed the suit was truly magnificent. Since early morning, people had been gathering to see the Emperor's new clothes in the parade.

The word had spread quickly, that only the wisest
among them could see the suit. So when the Emperor
paraded past wearing no clothes at all — not one of them seemed
to notice. And as not one of them wished to look a fool they
clapped and cheered the Emperor all through the town.

All at once a little boy in the front of the crowd pointed his finger at the Emperor and yelled, ''He's got no clothes on!''

A giggle went round the crowd when they realised how stupid they had been. Poor Emperor! His face turned very red, but he held his head up high and paraded slowly back to his Palace. He felt such a fool.

As for the two weavers — they left the Palace rather quickly, just before the parade started — perhaps they couldn't wait to spend all that gold!

# RUMPELSTILTSKIN

There was once a poor miller who had a beautiful daughter. He was so proud of her, that he talked about her all day long — to anyone who would listen. "She is a bride fit for the King himself," boasted the miller to his neighbours.

How they all laughed, which made the miller brag even more. "She can even spin straw into gold!" the miller shouted at the top of his voice.

Nobody believed him, of course, except one man. He was the King's huntsman who often rode past the mill.

On his return to the Palace, the huntsman told the King about the girl who could spin straw into gold. Now the King loved gold, and when he heard the huntsman's story, he ordered the miller's daughter to be brought before him at once.

The poor girl was horrified when she knew what her father had said. But she was too afraid to tell the King her father had lied.

The King led the trembling girl into a room filled with straw. "Spin this into gold before sunrise, or you will die," ordered the King. And he locked the door behind him.

In the corner of the room was a spinning wheel. The miller's daughter took one look at it and began to weep.

All of a sudden a strange little man jumped down from a tiny window high up in the wall. He took off his cap and bowed very low. "I won't tell you my name," he grinned. "Give me your necklace and I will gladly spin all this straw into gold for you." Straight away he sat down at the spinning wheel and never stopped until every last piece of straw was turned into gold.

In the morning when the King unlocked the door, the whole room was full of gold. The dwarf, of course, was nowhere to be seen.

The King was amazed and delighted with the miller's daughter.

"May I go back home to my father now?" the poor girl begged.

The King shook his head saying, "Rest here and have some food. You have worked all night and must be tired." The miller's daughter dare not disobey the King, so she had to stay.

Now this King was very greedy, and when he saw the pile of gold, he wanted more. So that night, when the miller's daughter woke up, he led her to an even bigger room piled high with straw, and locked her inside.

Once more the girl began to weep, and once more the little man appeared — eager to begin his spinning. This time he asked for her scarf in return for his work. And the girl gladly gave it to him.

In the morning when the King unlocked the door, the room was full of gold yet again. ''Spin one more room full of gold tonight,'' smiled the King, ''and I will make you my Queen,''

So that night the girl was locked in the biggest room in the Palace. It was full from floor to ceiling with straw.

Yet again the dwarf appeared. "I have nothing left to give in return for your work," sobbed the miller's daughter. Then the dwarf smiled a wicked smile. "Give me your first child when you are Queen," he laughed. What could the poor girl do but agree?

The dwarf worked hard all night. In the morning his task was done, and the room was packed with gold.

The King kept his promise and married the miller's daughter, and she became his Queen. They were very happy together, especially when a little daughter was born to them.

One day the Queen sat nursing her baby, when the dwarf suddenly appeared before her. "I've come for your first born child," the dwarf cackled, jumping up and down.

The Queen turned pale as she clutched the baby tightly in her arms. She had forgotten all about her promise to the crafty dwarf.

The Queen offered the dwarf jewels, money, anything in the whole Kingdom, but he refused.

However, when she cried so bitterly, he made a bargain with her. "If you can guess my name in three days — you may keep your child."

The Queen stayed awake all night, trying to remember all the names she had ever heard. Everybody in the Palace made long lists of every name they could think of.

On the first day, the dwarf
came back. The Queen told him
every name she knew, but after each
one the dwarf shouted, "That is not
my name!"

That night, the Queen secretly sent her
messengers all over the land, to collect new names.
When they returned to the palace at first light next
day, they had brought back hundreds.

When the dwarf returned for the second time, the Queen read every name her messengers had collected. After every one, the dwarf just laughed and shook his head. Not one of them was right.

By now the Queen was distraught. Only one more day left and everyone had run out of names. Soon the dwarf would take her precious little daughter.

Long before it was light on the third day, a messenger rode into the Palace courtyard demanding to see the Queen.

"I have not been able to find any new names, but I have a very strange tale to tell." He told the Queen how he had passed by a hut hidden deep in the woods. Outside the hut was a fire, round which a strange little man was singing:

"Flames dance, fire shine! Tomorrow, the Queen's child is mine. No more straw to gold I'll spin! For my name is Rumpelstiltskin!"

Can you imagine how happy the Queen was when she heard that name?

When the dwarf came back on the third day, the Queen pretended not to know, and guessed many names. Then she said with a smile, "Could it be Rumpelstiltskin?"

The dwarf was furious, he screamed and stamped with rage. Such was his fury, that he split right in two and vanished without a trace.

The King and the miller's daughter were happy for many years. Perhaps, when the baby Princess is older she will be told the story of the dwarf who could turn straw into gold.

# THE LITTLE TIN SOLDIER

Once upon a time, there lived an old toymaker. Folk came from miles around to gaze in his shop window full of toys, and sometimes they would call in and buy presents for their children.

One day, the old toymaker melted down a very large tin spoon. Carefully he poured the hot metal into some special moulds to make a set of tin soldiers. He filled up twenty of the moulds, but on the twenty-first he ran out of tin.

So when the soldiers were turned out, twenty were exactly alike — but the very last tin soldier had one leg missing.

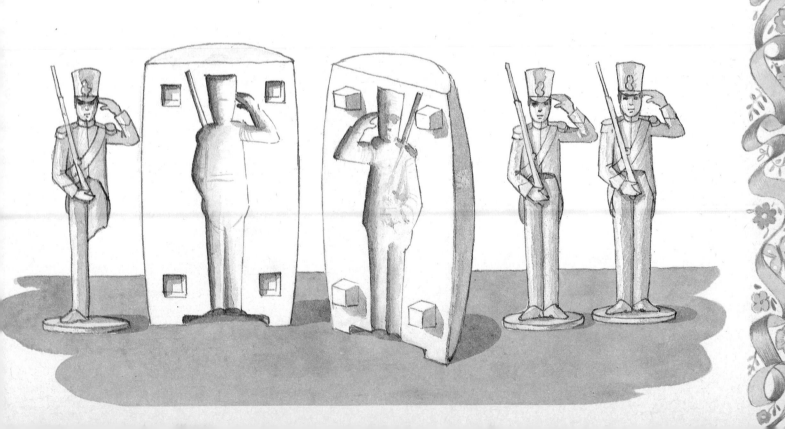

With great skill, the old toymaker painted the soldiers. He gave them red tunics and blue trousers and finished off their hats with gold braid. They looked splendid standing stiffly to attention and saluting. Even the tin soldier with one leg stood up just as straight as the others, looking every bit as brave and dashing. The old man was pleased with his work. And it wasn't too long before someone saw the twenty-one tin soldiers in his window, and bought them.

The box full of soldiers were given to a small boy for his birthday, and when he lifted the lid, he was thrilled to bits. "Tin soldiers," he gasped. "Just what I've always wanted."

The boy stood all his soldiers in a row in his nursery without even noticing that one of them had only one leg.

The little tin soldier gazed around him at the other toys. The floor below was littered with teddy bears, clockwork toys, bricks and dolls and a toy fort for the tin soldiers.

But the best toy was a splendid cardboard castle. It had tall pillars either side of the door, and more windows than the tin soldier could count. On the steps of the cardboard castle stood a graceful ballerina doll. She was balanced perfectly on one leg with the other stretched behind her — it looked as if she had only one leg.

"What a perfect wife she would make for me," sighed the little tin soldier as he gazed into her eyes. But the ballerina doll didn't even blink — she just stood there on one leg, staring back at the tin soldier. "I know that she is far too good for me," the tin soldier thought to himself. "But I must be very brave and look into her eyes until she speaks to me."

At night, when all the people in the house were asleep, the toys came out to play. The dolls and teddies danced and played games. The clockwork mice held races against the cars. Even the tin soldiers (who were supposed to be on guard) joined in the fun. But the little tin soldier and the ballerina doll just remained perfectly still and stared at each other.

Suddenly one night, the clock in the nursery struck midnight. The jack-in-the-box flew open and a bad tempered goblin flew out. He pointed a boney finger at the tin soldier. "Stop staring at the ballerina or it will be the worse for you," he snarled.

Although the goblin gave the tin soldier a terrible fright, he bravely stood to attention and continued to gaze at the ballerina doll.

Very early next morning the little boy came into his nursery to play with his soldiers. He lined them up in a row on the window ledge — then ran off to have his breakfast.

Without any warning, the little tin soldier was whisked through the air. He fell out of the open window, and down into the street below . . . who knows how it happened. It may have been just a gust of wind or even that nasty goblin. No-one will ever know!

As the poor tin soldier lay upside down in the gutter it began to pour with rain. Two little boys came running past, and one of them spotted the tin soldier. The other had made a paper boat, so they stood the soldier in the front and carefully launched it into the gutter.

Swiftly the boat sped along the water until it was swept into a deep drain beneath the street. The brave tin soldier showed no fear, even when the boat sailed out of the drain and into the river. Then it began to sink!

All too soon the water was up to the soldier's chest. The paper boat became so soggy that it just fell to pieces, and the tin soldier sank beneath the surface.

What a brave tin soldier he was! He showed no fear at all, even when the biggest fish in the river swallowed him up. It was terribly dark and gloomy inside the fish's stomach. The brave tin soldier kept his spirits up by thinking about the lovely ballerina — and how he must see her once more.

One day, the great fish
was caught with a rod and line,
and ended up on a kitchen table.
As the cook cut open the fish with
her sharp knife, the brave tin
soldier fell out onto the table. The
startled cook picked him up and
took him up to the nursery.

Now it was the tin soldier's
turn to be surprised. He found
himself in the very same nursery
with the very same toys: the dolls,
the teddies, all his soldier friends
— and best of all, his lovely
ballerina doll. They looked at
each other, but neither of them
said one word.

That night, when all was quiet, the brave tin soldier slowly made his way to the cardboard castle. He was going to beg the ballerina to come away with him.

As he reached her side the jack-in-the-box lid flew open, and the goblin pushed the brave tin soldier backwards. How dreadful! The poor tin soldier fell straight into the fire.

Then something very strange happened. The nursery door opened and the sudden draught blew the ballerina doll into the arms of the tin soldier. The fire flared up and they both melted away together in the flames.

Next morning, when the fire had cooled, the maid came to clear out the ashes. All she found was a little piece of tin in the shape of a heart.

# THUMBELINA

There was once a woman who lived all alone. Her cottage stood by itself in the heart of the countryside, far from neighbours and friends.

She was very lonely and longed for someone to keep her company. "I wish I had a little child of my own," the woman said out loud, as she worked in her garden.

It just so happened that an old witch was passing by and heard her. She fumbled in the folds of her cloak and took out one small seed, "This is a magic seed. Plant it and see what grows." And with that the witch vanished.

As the woman was very fond of flowers, she planted the seed carefully in a pot and placed it on her kitchen window.

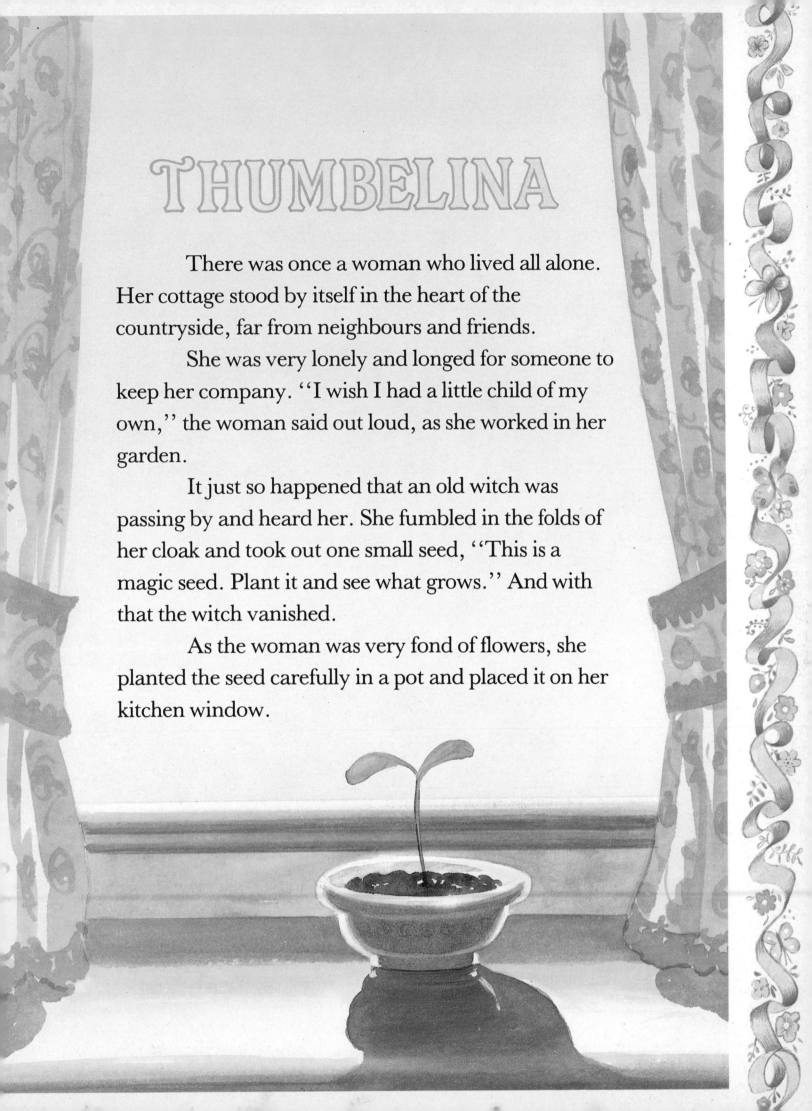

In no time at all, a green shoot appeared. By the next day a tall stalk had grown with a flower bud at the top.

When the woman bent down to admire it, the flower bud burst open. Sitting right in the middle of the petals was a tiny girl — no bigger than a thumb.

The woman smiled, "I think I shall call you, Thumbelina."

So tiny was the little girl, that half a walnut shell was just the right size for her bed. Her covers were made of rose petals with a soft rose bud for a pillow. A daisy made a perfect hat, and a violet leaf made a fine umbrella.

The woman took great care to see that her beloved Thumbelina came to no harm.

One warm night as she lay fast asleep in her walnut bed, an ugly toad peered through the window. "She'll make a perfect wife for my son," he croaked. And he grabbed Thumbelina in her walnut shell bed and jumped out of the window.

The ugly toad hopped and hopped far away through the darkness, taking great care not to wake little Thumbelina.

When he reached his home in the mud of the river bank, he showed Thumbelina to his son — who was twice as ugly as his father!

The two toads swam with the walnut shell bed into the middle of the river, and placed it on a lily pad. "Tomorrow you can get married," croaked the old toad to his son.

First thing next morning the toads returned. When Thumbelina peeped out of her bed and saw the ugly pair swimming towards her, she screamed with fright.

All at once, the lily pad began to move, swiftly it floated downstream far away from the angry toads.

Thumbelina had the fish in the river to thank for her lucky escape. They had overheard the toads' dreadful plan, and nibbled away at the lily pad to rescue her.

Thumbelina, still on her lily pad, floated swiftly downstream. At last she came to rest at the water's edge in the long grass.

Just at that moment, a big black beetle flew overhead. He swooped down and carried the tiny girl off into the wood to be his bride.

How the other beetles laughed when they saw Thumbelina. "Where are her wings?" the lady beetles cried. "And why has she got only two legs instead of six?" they scoffed.

All this jeering made the big black beetle feel ashamed of Thumbelina. So he flew away, leaving her alone in the wood.

Happily, the little girl soon found new friends all around her. Squirrels and rabbits came to her with their torn jackets and holey socks to mend. The birds and mice often asked her to baby-sit with their young ones. In return they brought her food. The bees buzzed by with honey and she found juicy berries and nuts everywhere.

All too soon autumn came. The days got shorter and the nights grew dark. Cold winds blew all the leaves from the trees, and Thumbelina shivered with cold in her thin clothes.

Most of her woodland friends had crept into their warm holes for their long winter sleep. Poor Thumbelina was all alone.

A few flakes of snow started to fall, just enough to cover the ground. But to tiny Thumbelina it seemed like deep drifts. Very soon she lost her balance and fell with a bump against a grassy bank.

"Who's that knocking on my door?" squeaked a friendly fieldmouse, as he held his lantern high. There in its bright beam he saw Thumbelina, shivering with cold and very hungry. "Come inside into my warm parlour and have some food, you poor creature," the fieldmouse said kindly.

Thumbelina liked the fieldmouse so much, and found his house so comfortable, that she agreed to stay all winter.

How quickly the winter months passed by. Thumbelina cooked and cleaned for the mouse, and in the long evenings she told him lovely stories.

One afternoon the field-mouse invited his neighbour, the mole, to tea. The tiny girl baked a chocolate cake, and took great care to serve the visitor properly.

The mole was a handsome fellow, with a black velvet coat and very good manners. To her great surprise, after he had eaten his last piece of cake, the mole asked Thumbelina to marry him.

"I don't want to marry anyone," cried Thumbelina with dismay.

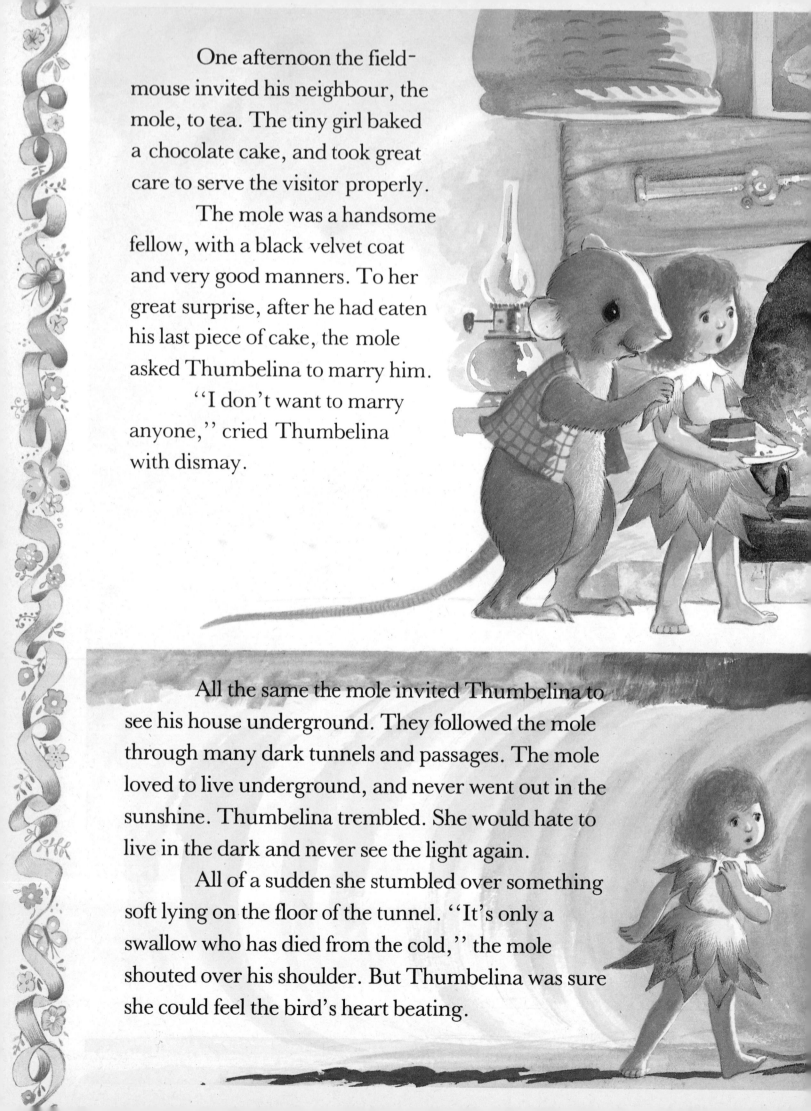

All the same the mole invited Thumbelina to see his house underground. They followed the mole through many dark tunnels and passages. The mole loved to live underground, and never went out in the sunshine. Thumbelina trembled. She would hate to live in the dark and never see the light again.

All of a sudden she stumbled over something soft lying on the floor of the tunnel. "It's only a swallow who has died from the cold," the mole shouted over his shoulder. But Thumbelina was sure she could feel the bird's heart beating.

Later that night, when the fieldmouse was asleep, she fetched a blanket and some warm milk, which soon made the swallow feel better.

She cared for him all winter long. And when spring came, he was ready to fly away.

The swallow pleaded with Thumbelina to fly away with him. "If only I could," she sighed. "But the fieldmouse has begged me to marry the mole tomorrow. He has been so good and kind to me — that I must agree." So sadly the two friends parted.

Feeling very unhappy, Thumbelina asked the fieldmouse if she might go out in the sunshine for the last time before she married the mole.

As she stepped outside, the swallow swept down from the sky. This was her last chance of freedom. Thumbelina jumped on the bird's back and the swallow carried her home to her cottage.

At long last everyone was together again and happy once more.

# SINBAD

Once upon a time, in the faraway city of Bagdad, there lived a young man whose name was Sinbad. He longed for adventure, and that is why he sailed the seven seas.

One day, Sinbad sailed away on one of many journeys. After many days at sea, his ship dropped anchor at a tiny island, and Sinbad and the other sailors stepped ashore to look around.

All at once, the island seemed to grow and rise up out of the water. It was no island, but a monster whale! Suddenly, the whale took a great dive beneath the waves, and everyone fell off into the sea.

All the other sailors managed to swim back to the ship, but poor Sinbad was left behind floating in the water, clinging to a piece of driftwood.

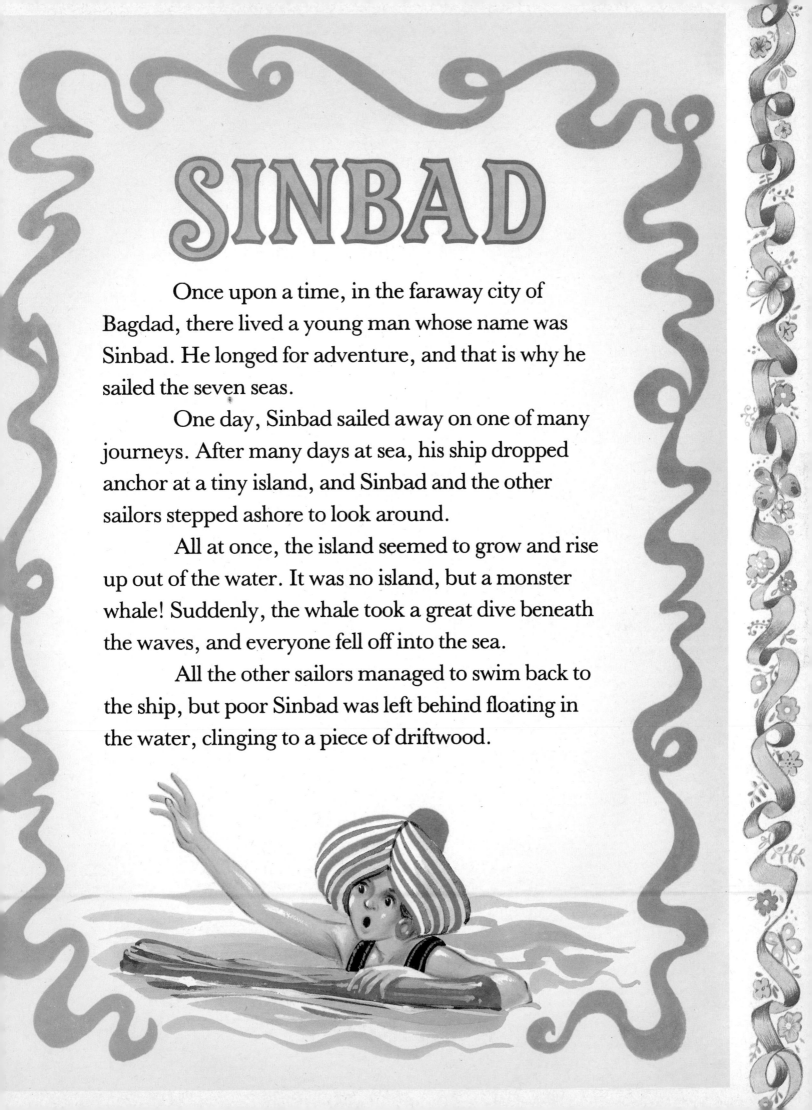

After a while he was washed ashore on another island. He ran across the sandy beach and climbed the tallest palm tree, to try to see his ship. But alas, Sinbad had been left all alone, and his ship was nowhere to be seen.

As he gazed down from the tree, Sinbad noticed a huge white egg on the sand. He slid down the trunk to take a better look. All of a sudden, a big black shadow passed over him. There, circling overhead, was a great white bird — almost as big as the island.

"Now's my chance to escape," thought Sinbad. And when the great white bird flew down onto its egg, Sinbad unwound his turban and tied himself onto the bird's gigantic leg.

Sure enough, the bird flew off carrying Sinbad with him. His plan had worked.

The great bird flew high in the air, through deep valleys and over mountains, until it landed at last, and Sinbad could untie his turban and escape.

The boy found himself in a dry river bed, surrounded by steep cliffs too difficult to climb. He was trapped again.

"How did I get myself into this mess?" Sinbad cried out loudly, and his voice echoed round the cliffs.

All of a sudden, there came a loud hissing noise. All around poor Sinbad large serpents slithered across the floor. Underneath the snakes were huge diamonds and gems — some as big as Sinbad himself.

At the sight of so much treasure, Sinbad's eyes opened wide. Then he remembered the snakes and ran to the nearest cave for safety.

"I can hear voices," cried Sinbad in delight. "Someone is here to rescue me." The boy looked up and saw faces peering over the edge of the cliffs. Men were throwing something onto the rocks below. Could it be huge pieces of meat?

At once, Sinbad understood what was happening. These men threw lumps of meat onto the diamonds near the snakes, then the mountain eagles would swoop down, grab the meat, and carry it back to their nests. Sometimes a few of the diamonds would stick to the meat, and then the men would grab the gems from the eagles' nests.

Sinbad waited for the biggest bird to swoop down. He grabbed the largest diamond he could find and clung onto the bird's legs with all his might.

And that is how our adventurer, Sinbad, escaped the snakes. And that is how he came to be sitting in an eagle's nest with the biggest diamond of them all.

Sinbad returned home a rich man. After a while he got tired of doing nothing and made up his mind to set sail on another voyage.

After many days at sea, his ship dropped anchor in the harbour of a large city.

When the people saw Sinbad and his crew, they begged him for help. ''Our markets are quite empty of fruit. We have nothing to sell and nothing to buy,'' they moaned. ''We have no coconuts or dates, no pomegranates or figs — not even one banana.''

Sinbad looked puzzled, until the people explained, ''Our trees are so tall and smooth, it is impossible for anyone to climb them, except the monkeys.''

"Leave it to us," laughed Sinbad and his sailors. And they set off to find the trees in the forest.

When the ship's crew saw the monkeys who lived in the top branches, it gave them an idea. The sailors looked around for stones, which they threw at the monkeys — who thought it was some sort of game. The mischievous monkeys pelted the sailors with coconuts and fruit, who, in turn, filled up great sacks with them.

They returned to the city and gave the food to the hungry people. Everyone was very grateful and Sinbad and his crew sailed away with many presents and thanks from the city.

No sooner had Sinbad gone back home to Bagdad, than the Caliph sent for him. "Set sail at once," he commanded, "and take these gifts to my friend the Sultan of Tasmir Island."

So once more, Sinbad and his crew put to sea — but alas, on the way, the ship was attacked by pirates, who captured all on board. At the very next port these cruel pirates sold Sinbad and his crew as slaves.

Sinbad was bought by a wealthy merchant who had a lovely daughter. "Slave," grinned the merchant, "I have a very dangerous task for you," and he dragged Sinbad deep into the forest.

"In a few moments the biggest elephant in the world will pass this way to drink at the river. Take this bow and arrow and shoot him," and at that, the merchant pushed Sinbad up the tree and ran away.

All at once, Sinbad could feel the trees shaking. Thundering down the path came an enormous elephant with gleaming tusks. Sinbad shook with fright!

The poor boy trembled so much that he lost his balance and fell out of the tree. He landed on top of the elephant and slid down his trunk onto the ground. Sinbad closed his eyes tight, for he was certain the elephant's great foot would crush him to pulp.

A soft voice was speaking to the great elephant, it was the merchant's daughter. She was standing in the middle of the forest path — feeding him bread and fruit from a silver dish.

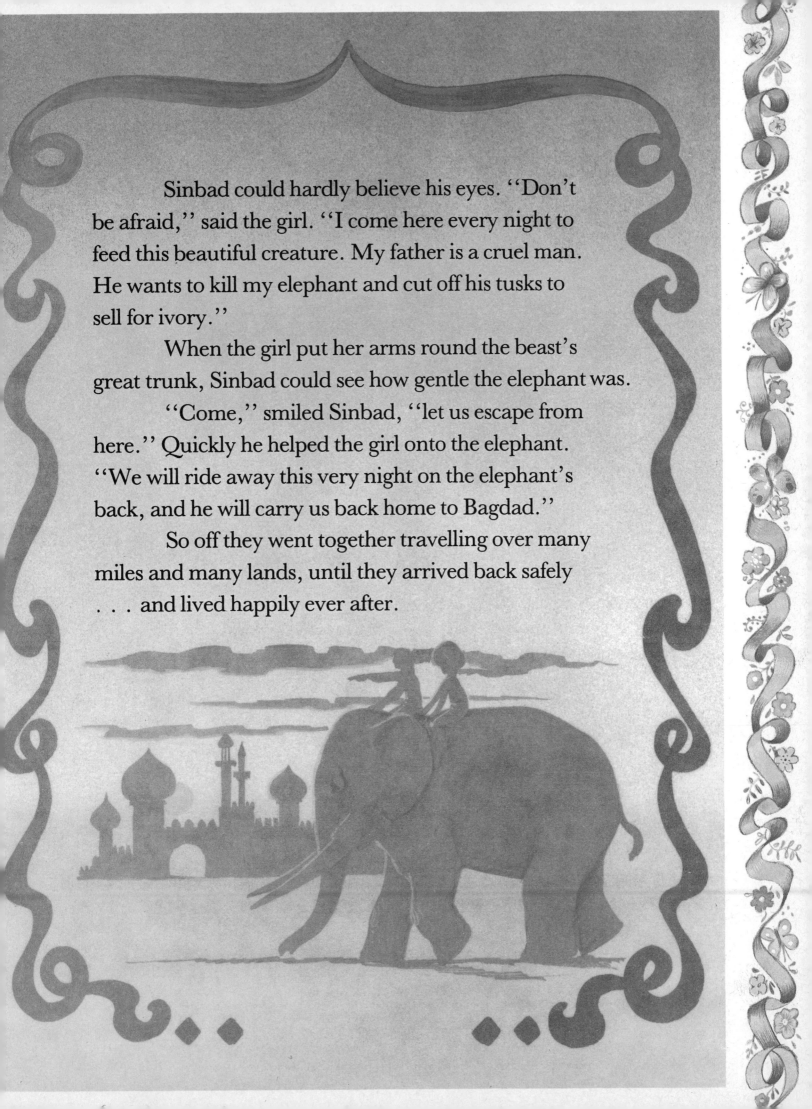

Sinbad could hardly believe his eyes. "Don't be afraid," said the girl. "I come here every night to feed this beautiful creature. My father is a cruel man. He wants to kill my elephant and cut off his tusks to sell for ivory."

When the girl put her arms round the beast's great trunk, Sinbad could see how gentle the elephant was.

"Come," smiled Sinbad, "let us escape from here." Quickly he helped the girl onto the elephant. "We will ride away this very night on the elephant's back, and he will carry us back home to Bagdad."

So off they went together travelling over many miles and many lands, until they arrived back safely . . . and lived happily ever after.

# THE THREE LITTLE PIGS

Once upon a time, there was a Mother Pig who lived on a farm with her three little piglets, in a warm and comfortable sty.

They were very happy together and got on very well with all the other animals. The farmer gave them plenty to eat. He filled up their trough twice a day with as many turnips and juicy apples as they could manage.

As you may know, pigs are very fond of their food — so it came as no surprise when the little pigs grew too large for the farmyard.

Mother Pig gazed at them with pride, "You have grown so big now, that you must go out into the world and build new houses for yourselves."

As they waved goodbye, their mother gave them some good advice. "Always remember," she said with a tear in her eye, "to beware of the Big Bad Wolf." So, off the three little pigs went, singing and whistling down the road.

Before very long, they came to a stack of straw. "It must be my lucky day," chuckled the first little pig. "I shall build my house with straw, right on this very spot!" Quickly, he gathered up the straw — and in next to no time he had built himself a little house.

The second little pig trotted on until he came
to a wood. "How very fortunate I am," giggled the
second little pig. "I shall build my house with sticks.
This is a good place to live, and I shan't have to carry
them far."

So, he set to work and soon had a fine wooden
house, with windows and doors and even a wooden
chimney. The second little pig felt quite safe from the
Big Bad Wolf, so he settled down to eat his dinner.

Now, the third little pig was much wiser than the other two. He planned to build his house of bricks — and had brought along the tools to do the job. He worked very hard for a long time before his house was finished and he was safe inside.

All this time, the Big Bad Wolf had been keeping his eye on the three little pigs.

Sure enough, one dreadful day, the Big Bad Wolf came knocking on the first little pig's door and said, "Little pig, little pig, can I come in?"

"Not by the hair on my chinny chin chin, you cannot come in," squealed the first little pig.

"Then I'll huff and I'll puff and I'll blow your house down," said the wolf. So he huffed and he puffed, and in no time at all the straw house had blown away — and the wolf gobbled up the first little pig.

Next day, the wolf went to see where the second little pig lived. It didn't take him long to find the house made of sticks. When the second little pig heard the wolf coming, he hurried inside and locked the door.

The Big Bad Wolf banged on the door and cried, "Little pig, little pig, can I come in?"

"Not by the hair on my chinny chin chin, you cannot come in," squealed the second little pig.

"Then I'll huff and I'll puff and I'll blow your house down," said the wolf. So he huffed and he puffed, and in no time at all, the stick house just fell to pieces — and the wolf gobbled up the second little pig.

It wasn't very long before the wolf found the brick house built by the third little pig. He marched up the path and banged on the door, "Little pig, little pig, can I come in?"

"Not by the hair on my chinny chin chin, you cannot come in," shouted the third little pig.

"Then I'll huff and I'll puff and I'll blow your house down," said the wolf. So he huffed and he puffed — but the brick house did not fall down.

The furious wolf ran at the house and banged and kicked the walls — trying to knock them down. But still the brick house did not fall in. So the wolf had to give up and go home.

"I haven't seen the last of him," the little pig thought to himself. And, of course, he was right.

That crafty wolf made his mind up to trick the last little pig and make a tasty meal of him. So the very next day the wolf shouted through the little pig's window, "Come with me tomorrow morning at six o'clock and we will dig some turnips for ourselves from the farmer's field."

But, the clever little pig got up an hour early, and when the wolf called for him, he was back safe inside his brick house, eating the turnips.

Then, the wolf said, "Meet me at five tomorrow morning and we can pick apples together from that tree over there."

At four the next morning, the little pig climbed
the tree to pick apples. But just as he reached the top,
he saw the wolf waiting underneath — ready to eat
him.

"These apples are so juicy," called the little
pig, throwing one far from the tree. And while the
wolf ran after the apple, the clever little pig jumped
down and ran all the way home.

Still that Big Bad Wolf wouldn't give up.
"Come with me to the fair at four this afternoon," he
begged the little pig.

So at two o'clock the third little pig trotted off to the fair to ride on the roundabouts and swings. As he had some money left, he bought himself a butterchurn.

On his way home, as he reached the top of the hill, he spied the wolf coming towards him. So he jumped inside the butterchurn.

It toppled over and began to roll down the hill. Faster and faster it went, until it rolled right over the wolf and knocked him flat. The little pig ran home, shaken, but safe and sound.

Later that night the little pig heard a noise on
his roof! It was the Big Bad Wolf!

"I am going to climb down your chimney and
eat you up," the wolf shouted, as he began to climb down.

Quick as he could, the little pig took the lid off
a huge pot boiling on his fire. The Big Bad Wolf came
sliding down the chimney and fell with a splash
straight into the boiling pot.

And that, I'm happy to say, was the end of him.

But it wasn't the end of the third little pig. He
was far too clever for that Big Bad Wolf.

# THE UGLY DUCKLING

It was summertime. The sky was blue and the air was filled with the scent of meadow flowers — and the sound of bees buzzing from flower to flower made Mother Duck feel very sleepy.

She had been sitting on her nest all summer long, hidden deep in the reeds on the edge of a pond. The Mother Duck felt rather lonely all by herself. "I do wish my ducklings would hatch," she sighed, "then I would have someone to talk to and join me in a dip in the pond."

At long last the eggs began to crack open. First one, then another and another, until all the ducklings had popped out of their shells. Their soft yellow down soon dried out in the warm summer sun. In next to no time they were all eager to discover their new world.

The baby ducklings jumped out of their nest and ran into the reeds. Some of them hid, and of course, some of them got lost. ''Peep, peep! What a big world,'' they all cried darting everywhere. Poor Mother Duck felt quite muddled.

"A bit of peace and quiet is what I need," she quacked as she waddled back to her nest to rest. It was then she noticed one egg that had not hatched. "How strange," she thought. "This egg is so big, it doesn't look like mine at all."

But she sat down all the same, just to keep it warm. At last the big egg cracked. Out tumbled a duckling twice as big as the rest. Sad to say compared to the others, he could only be described as ugly.

Poor Mother Duck shook her feathers as she gazed at her huge duckling, "How big and ugly you are. Not a bit like the others."

It was time to take her new family down to the pond for a swim. One by one the ducklings jumped into the water with a splash. Then up they bobbed, swimming along beautifully — especially the Ugly Duckling.

How quickly they could swim across the pond, following their mother in a straight line. "What a wonderful place the world is," cheeped the ducklings. Then one by one they hopped out of the pond and into the farmyard.

What a noisy place it was. Full of ducks and hens pushing and pecking at each other, and fighting over every scrap of food in the place.

Sad to say, nobody liked the Ugly Duckling. Perhaps it was because he was different, and not soft and fluffy like all the other baby birds.

"He's so ugly," clucked one old hen. "I've never seen anything so awkward in all my days." And she tried to peck the Ugly Duckling's legs.

This made the poor duckling feel terribly unhappy. "I am so ugly. I will go far away so no-one can look at me."

So he ran through the fields until he came to the marshes where the wild ducks lived. But he found no welcome there! They hissed at him and stabbed at him with their black beaks until he ran away again.

As darkness fell the Ugly Duckling came to an old cottage. He crept under the door and stayed all night in the warmth. Next morning an old woman with a cat and a hen found him. "Can you lay duck eggs?" she asked. The Ugly Duckling shook his head.

"Then you'll have to go," snarled the cat as he chased him out the door.

And so the Ugly Duckling made up his mind to find a place to hide where no-one would see how ugly he was. For weeks and weeks he lived alone by a lake. Summer had gone and winter was on its way.

One evening a flock of lovely white birds flew overhead. The duckling gazed up at them in wonder. ''If only I could be as beautiful as that!'' and he began to cry.

That night was so cold that the lake turned to ice. The Ugly Duckling was so tired he fell asleep and froze fast to the ice.

Very early next day, luckily for the
Ugly Duckling, a passing farmer found him. He
cracked the ice with his stick and freed the duckling.
He pushed him inside his warm jacket and carried
him home to his wife.

"I could fatten him up,"
she said. "In a few weeks he'll
make a fine roast dinner."

Unfortunately, the farmer's
two children were very naughty.
All day long they chased the
duckling round the kitchen trying
to grab him.

One dreadful day they
chased him so much that he flew
into a milk churn. The farmer's
wife screamed and almost hit him
with the poker. He tried to escape
but landed right in the middle of a
barrel of flour.

In the upset that followed,
the Ugly Duckling darted out of the
kitchen door, and never stopped
until he reached a peaceful lake.

There he stayed, sad and lonely all winter
long, until spring came.

Somehow the warm sun made the duckling
feel glad to be alive. As he swam out of his hiding place
in the reeds, three snow white swans glided towards him.

The Ugly Duckling bowed his head, waiting for them to peck and hiss at him. It was then he saw his reflection in the water.

No longer was he a big clumsy Ugly Duckling — but a graceful white swan.

''Fly away with us,'' said the swans. So, happy at last, the new swan spread his wings and flew away with them across the lake.

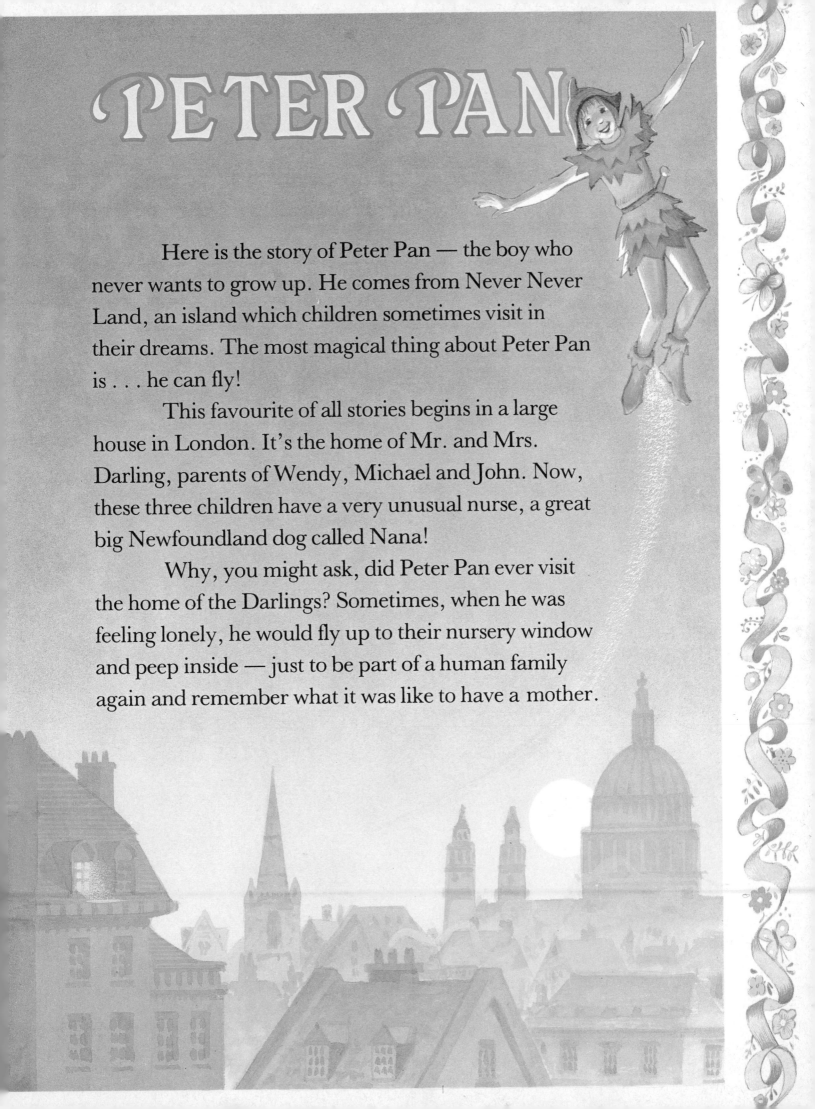

# PETER PAN

Here is the story of Peter Pan — the boy who never wants to grow up. He comes from Never Never Land, an island which children sometimes visit in their dreams. The most magical thing about Peter Pan is . . . he can fly!

This favourite of all stories begins in a large house in London. It's the home of Mr. and Mrs. Darling, parents of Wendy, Michael and John. Now, these three children have a very unusual nurse, a great big Newfoundland dog called Nana!

Why, you might ask, did Peter Pan ever visit the home of the Darlings? Sometimes, when he was feeling lonely, he would fly up to their nursery window and peep inside — just to be part of a human family again and remember what it was like to have a mother.

If the nursery window was left open and Nana the dog was nowhere about, Peter would fly right into the nursery. Wendy often caught a glimpse of the strange boy — but she thought she was just dreaming.

Now one night, Mrs. Darling was sitting sewing while her children slept. Peter flew straight in through the window. He didn't notice that Nana was in the nursery. The dog sprang up and growled and snarled at the boy. As he tried to escape, his shadow caught on the window — and Peter had to leave it behind. Rather startled, Mrs. Darling picked it up and put it in a drawer.

The very next evening when the Darlings were out, a tiny bright light flew in through the window and began to dart about — it was Tinker Bell, a tiny fairy who went everywhere with Peter Pan.

She was searching for Peter's shadow. She looked in all the cupboards, all the drawers, she even delved inside a jug. Eventually she found the right place just as Peter flew in through the window.

He grabbed his shadow and shut the drawer tight, trapping poor Tinker Bell inside. He searched around trying to find something that would stick his shadow back on.

All this noise woke up Wendy. She knew what to do straight away. She fetched her workbox, and very neatly stitched the shadow on again.

When Wendy offered Peter a kiss he looked puzzled. He had never had a kiss before and held his hand out for a present. So Wendy gave him her silver thimble instead. In return, Peter gave her one of his acorn-shaped buttons, which Wendy hung on a chain round her neck.

As Peter sat in the nursery he told Wendy all about Never Never Land where he lived with the Lost Boys and the fairies. He explained to her how a fairy dies every time a human child says, ''I do not believe in fairies!''

It was then that Peter remembered Tinker Bell still trapped in the drawer. He let her out, and she was furious. She buzzed round Wendy and tried to pull her hair. Perhaps she was jealous of Peter's new friend!

All this noise woke up John and Michael. They listened spellbound when Peter told them about his fierce fights with the Pirates on Never Never Land. And, of course they wanted to go.

So it was agreed that they should first learn to fly, and go away with Peter Pan that very night.

After a great deal of practise they were ready. Not a moment too soon, for running up the stairs came Mr. and Mrs. Darling.

One by one the children flew out of the nursery window, leaving their poor parents behind. Soon they were soaring through the night sky with the lights of London far below them.

On and on they went. "Second star to the right and on until morning," cried Peter Pan as he sped ahead.

At long last, as the sun rose, they glimpsed Never Never Land beneath them. It was just as Peter had said. Anchored near the island was the Pirate ship, Jolly Roger, with its evil Captain Hook. The Pirate chief hated Pan because he had cut off his hand and thrown it to the crocodile, who longed to eat the rest of him. Luckily the crocodile had swallowed a clock, and everyone could hear him coming with his loud, tick, tick, tick.

As they flew over the island, Wendy and the boys saw an Indian tribe round their wigwams. These were the Indians who were always on the trail of the evil pirates.

Suddenly there came the most enormous bang. The Pirate ship below had fired its cannon. The blast scattered the children in different directions. Tinker Bell hated Wendy so much that she pretended to guide her to safety — instead she led her into terrible danger.

Below on the island, Peter's Lost Boys were looking up into the sky. They saw Wendy and thought she was a bird. "Peter wants you to shoot Wendy," cried Tinker Bell.

So the biggest boy took his bow and arrow and shot Wendy through the heart. She fluttered down from the sky and landed on the ground. Luckily the arrow had stuck into the acorn-shaped button Peter had given her, and she was quite unharmed.

Peter was so angry, he banished the wicked Tinker Bell for a whole week, which made her hate Wendy even more.

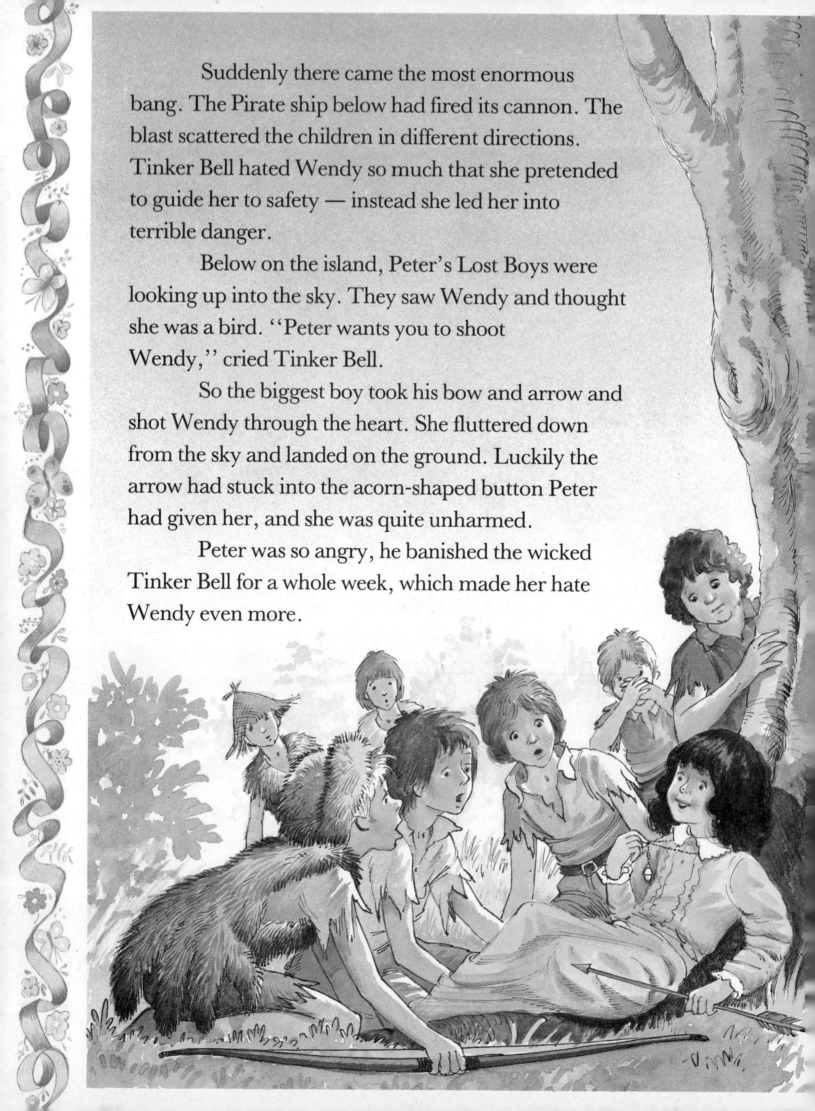

Eagerly the Lost Boys led Wendy to their secret home underground. To reach it, they squeezed through holes in certain tree trunks, then slid down into a huge cave below.

Wendy, John and Michael lived with the Lost Boys for weeks. Wendy did their washing, cooked all their meals, and told them stories like a real mother. She told such lovely stories about her home and her mother, that John and Michael wanted to go back home. The Lost Boys begged to be allowed to go there too.

This hurt Peter's feelings. He was afraid to leave Never Never Land for good, in case he grew up. However, he told Tinker Bell to guide them back home over the sea. Then sadly he shook hands with Wendy.

''Promise you will drink your glass of medicine every night when I am gone.'' The words were hardly out of her mouth, when the air was filled with a bloodcurdling scream.

The Pirates were attacking the Redskins in the forest above the Lost Boys' home. It was a bitter battle, and sad to say, the Pirates won. The Lost Boys, however, thought their friends the Redskins had won. So one by one they climbed out of their secret cave.

The evil Pirates were waiting, they pounced on them and captured them all. They tied everyone up and took them aboard the Jolly Roger.

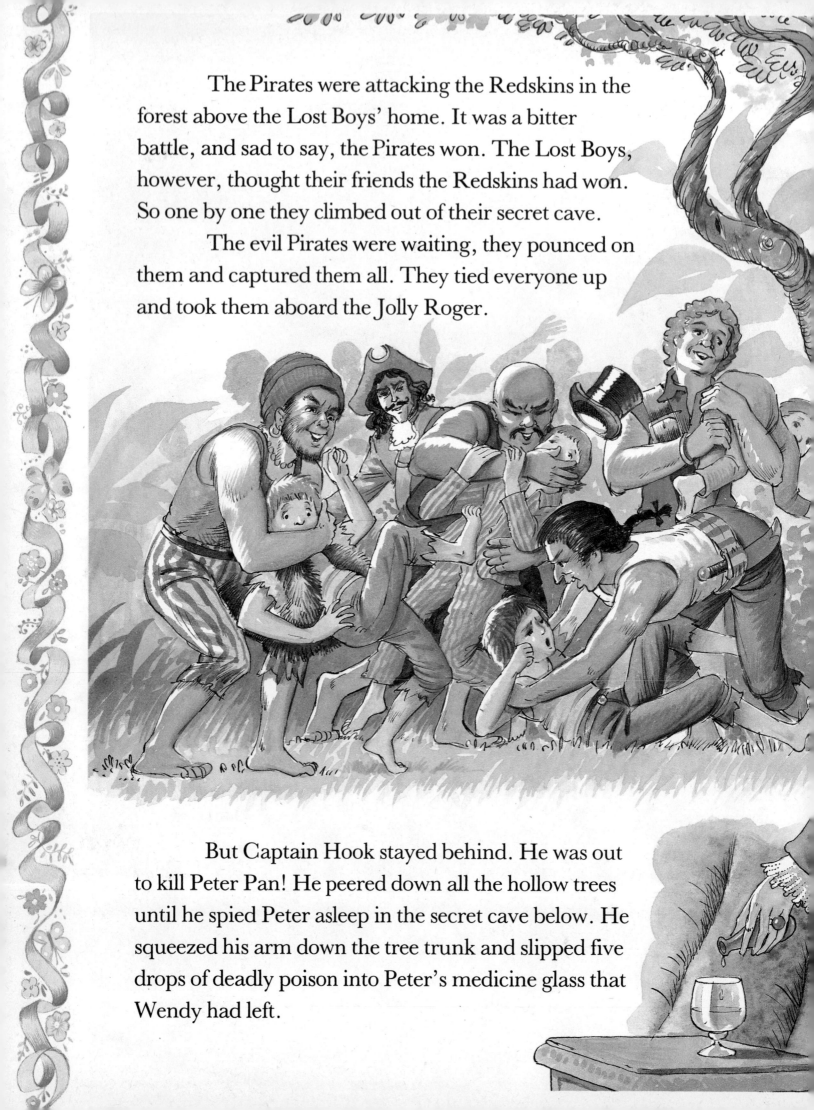

But Captain Hook stayed behind. He was out to kill Peter Pan! He peered down all the hollow trees until he spied Peter asleep in the secret cave below. He squeezed his arm down the tree trunk and slipped five drops of deadly poison into Peter's medicine glass that Wendy had left.

Later that night, Peter was woken up by Tinker Bell, who told him of Wendy's capture. Quickly, Peter jumped out of bed to take his medicine as he had promised. Tinker Bell knew it was deadly poison — as she had heard Captain Hook talking about it in the forest.

Bravely she flew up to the glass and drank the medicine herself. As she fell to the floor, her tiny fairy light was almost gone. She was going to die.

Peter stood up and shouted in his loudest voice, ''If you believe in fairies, clap your hands.'' It seemed as if the whole air was full of noise — made by all the children in the world. Tinker Bell was saved!

The evil Captain Hook had tied Wendy to the mast and was about to make the Lost Boys walk the plank. All at once he stopped. He fell on the deck in fear. "Tick, tick, tick." He thought it was the crocodile.

In fact it was Peter Pan imitating it. While Hook was hiding in fear, Peter slipped on board and freed everybody.

Then began the terrible fight with Hook. They clashed swords up and down the deck of the ship, until at last, Hook overbalanced and fell into the sea — where his friend the crocodile was waiting.

What joy it was for Wendy, John and Michael to return home. How happy the Darlings were to see their children home safely.

It is said that the Darlings adopted all the Lost Boys, and that Wendy goes back to Never Never Land every year to see Peter Pan — perhaps you may go there one day too!

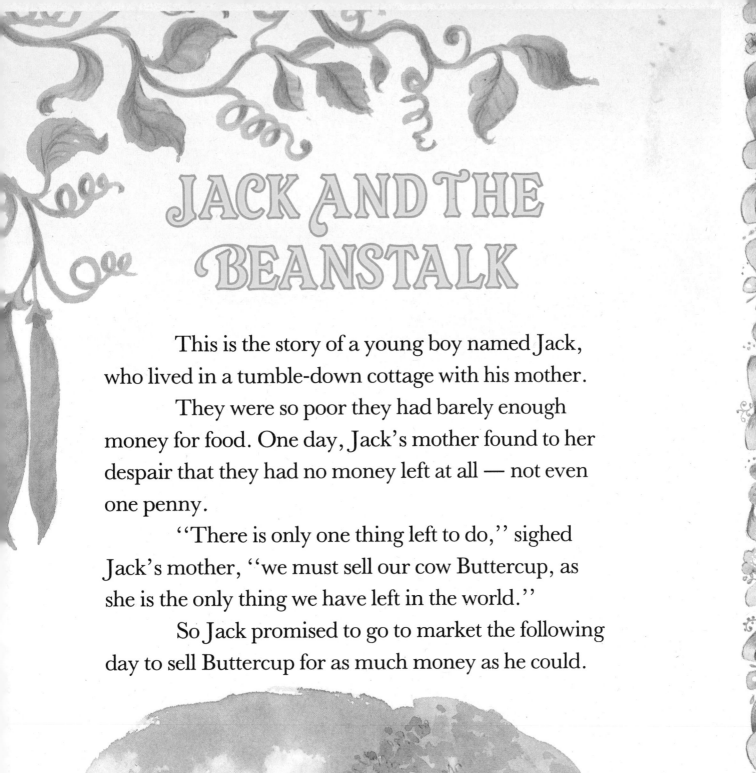

# JACK AND THE BEANSTALK

This is the story of a young boy named Jack, who lived in a tumble-down cottage with his mother.

They were so poor they had barely enough money for food. One day, Jack's mother found to her despair that they had no money left at all — not even one penny.

''There is only one thing left to do,'' sighed Jack's mother, ''we must sell our cow Buttercup, as she is the only thing we have left in the world.''

So Jack promised to go to market the following day to sell Buttercup for as much money as he could.

Early next morning before it was light, Jack left for market. He crept out of the house while his mother was still asleep. She was very fond of the cow, and would have found it hard to say goodbye.

Jack hadn't gone very far along the road before he met a pedlar.

"I will buy your cow in exchange for these five magic beans," the stranger said as he held out his hand. "Plant them and you will grow rich."

Young Jack couldn't resist. He gave Buttercup to the pedlar, grabbed the magic beans, and ran home to tell his mother.

She was rather surprised to see him back from market so soon. When she heard about the magic beans, she was so angry she tossed them out of the window. And poor silly Jack was sent to bed without any supper.

The next morning dawned dark and gloomy. Jack jumped out of bed and looked out of the window. The sky above was dark — not with clouds — but with giant green leaves! To Jack's amazement the magic beans had grown in the night. They were so tall, they covered the tiny cottage and disappeared up into the sky.

Jack had to push open the cottage door with all his might, he stepped outside and began to climb the beanstalk. The branches of the bean plant were so thick they formed a ladder, and soon Jack had climbed so high that his cottage was just a tiny speck down below.

At last the branches grew thinner and Jack knew he had reached the top. Ahead of him was a long road, which led to a mysterious castle in the distance. Bravely, Jack marched along until he reached the castle door. Loudly he knocked and waited.

It was opened by the most enormous woman Jack had ever seen. "Come in and eat," her great voice boomed. "Beware my husband the Giant — or he will eat you!"

Jack turned pale. "Don't be afraid," laughed the Giantess as she led Jack into her kitchen. The kind woman gave him a plate of food almost as high as himself. Jack had only taken two mouthfuls, when the whole room began to shake.

"My husband the Giant is home," cried the Giantess, and with that, she pushed Jack into the cupboard.

Not a moment too soon, for when the Giant strode into the room, he began to sniff around Jack's cupboard:

"Fee, fi, fo, fum,
I smell the blood of an Englishman;
Be he alive or be he dead,
I'll grind his bones to make my bread."

His wife smiled, "It's only the giant meat pie I cooked for your dinner that you can smell."

When he had gobbled up every scrap of food,
the Giant hammered on the table with his great fists.
"Wife," he called, "bring me my hen that lays golden eggs."

Jack could hardly believe his eyes when he
peeped out of the cupboard.

"Lay golden eggs," commanded the Giant.
And the little brown hen, which the Giant had placed
on the table, began to lay golden eggs. The Giant
scooped up the eggs, put them in his pocket and fell
fast asleep.

Jack saw his chance. He
jumped out of the cupboard,
snatched up the hen and ran for
his life until he reached the top
of the beanstalk.

He slid down the thick branches at top speed. His mother was overjoyed to see him back safe and sound. The little brown hen laid lots of eggs and made their fortune. Jack bought their cow Buttercup back and all three of them were very happy.

After a while, Jack longed to climb the beanstalk once more. So early one morning, before anyone could stop him, he climbed it again in search of adventure. Higher and higher he went, until he saw the winding road he knew led to the Giant's castle. Once again the castle door was opened by the Giant's wife. She didn't recognise Jack because of his fine new clothes, so she asked him in.

No sooner had Jack reached the kitchen, than the Giant returned. Jack looked around in panic.

"Hide in the log basket by the oven," begged the Giant's frightened wife.

Sure enough, the Giant strode straight over to where Jack was hiding.

"Fee, fi, fo, fum,

I smell the blood of an Englishman;

Be he alive or be he dead,

I'll grind his bones to make my bread."

"It's only the soup I made for you this morning," said his wife, as she placed the huge bowl on the table in front of him.

What a noise the Giant made drinking his soup! As soon as he had finished, he took down a beautiful golden harp from the shelf above him. ''Play me a lullaby,'' the Giant commanded the golden harp.

Jack had never heard such lovely music in his life. He knew he must have the harp for his very own. Such sweet music came from the harp, that the Giant soon fell into a deep sleep.

Jack saw his chance and seized the harp from the table. But as he ran out of the castle gates, the harp began to play loudly, ''Help me, Master. Help me!''

The Giant awoke just in time to see Jack disappearing with his harp out of the castle gates. He thundered after the boy, screaming and roaring: ''You stole my hen — you shall not have my golden harp!'' And he chased Jack towards the beanstalk.

Jack slid down the branches in fear of his life. He could feel the beanstalk swaying and cracking as the Giant began to climb down after him. Now the Giant was as slow as Jack was nimble. So, when the boy reached the bottom of the beanstalk, he grabbed an axe and chopped at the branches with all his might.

The whole thing began to sway. With a few more blows of Jack's axe, the whole beanstalk came crashing down — bringing the Giant with it. His great weight made a huge hole in the ground, into which he vanished and was never seen again!

Jack and his mother lived happily ever after, together with the golden harp the little brown hen, and of course, their cow named Buttercup!

# THE PRINCESS AND THE PEA

Once upon a time, there was a young Prince who decided to get married. "You must marry a real, genuine Princess," insisted his mother the Queen. "She must be beautiful, clever, charming and kind. Nothing less will do!" And with that, she ordered the Prince's horse to be saddled and told him to ride off and start looking at once.

As there were no Princesses in his own kingdom, the Prince had to travel to every country in the world to look for one.

He met lots of them on his journey, but not one was perfect. Some were too tall and some were much too small, others too fat and some too thin. Some were very old and some were just babies.

The poor Prince was really disappointed. "I just can't seem to find a real, genuine Princess anywhere," he sighed. So, he climbed on his horse and began the long ride back to his kingdom. When, at last, he returned home, he decided to give up the idea altogether.

One dark night there
was the most terrible storm.
The wind howled and rain fell
by the bucketful. Great flashes
of lightning lit up the sky, and
thunder shook the Palace walls.

In spite of all this noise,
the King heard the tiniest knock
on the Palace door.

"Now, who can be calling on a night like
this?" snorted the Queen, for she was warm and
comfortable and did not want to be disturbed.
However, the kindly old King got up from his chair
and went to open the door himself.

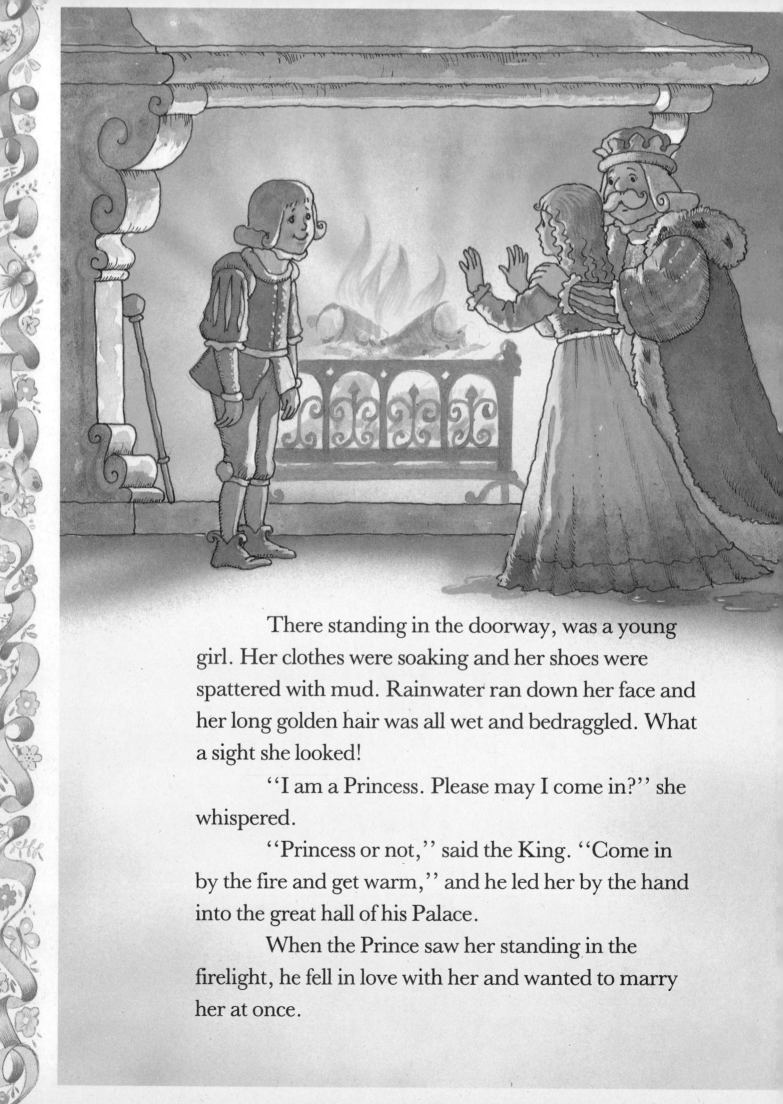

There standing in the doorway, was a young girl. Her clothes were soaking and her shoes were spattered with mud. Rainwater ran down her face and her long golden hair was all wet and bedraggled. What a sight she looked!

"I am a Princess. Please may I come in?" she whispered.

"Princess or not," said the King. "Come in by the fire and get warm," and he led her by the hand into the great hall of his Palace.

When the Prince saw her standing in the firelight, he fell in love with her and wanted to marry her at once.

The Queen took one look at the girl dripping water on her best carpet and frowned. "She can't be a real, genuine Princess and look such a mess," she muttered to herself. "I've never heard such a tale in all my life!"

With that, she marched off towards the Palace kitchens. And there, from the store cupboard, she took one tiny dried pea. Then she crept quietly up the back stairs into the very best guest room.

"We'll soon see if she's a real, genuine Princess," and she placed the pea right in the centre of the Princess's bed.

Next, the Queen sent for all the maids in the Palace. "Bring me twenty mattresses from your linen cupboard at once."

The maids looked surprised, but were soon scurrying up and down the corridors puffing and panting under the weight of all those mattresses.

"Pile them up high on the bed!" yelled the Queen. "Now fetch me twenty of your softest feather quilts," the Queen ordered in her sternest voice. So the maids brought the feather quilts. By now everyone was quite out of breath.

"Now place the twenty feather quilts on top of the twenty mattresses," the Queen went on.

The pile of mattresses was so high that the maids could no longer reach them. So the Queen ordered her pageboys to bring long ladders. They pulled the twenty quilts up the ladders until, at last, the job was done and the Queen was satisfied.

While all this was going on the Princess had dried out from her soaking and was ready for bed.

She climbed up the ladder right to the top of the twenty mattresses and twenty feather quilts.

''Now we shall see if she is a real, genuine Princess,'' smiled the Queen.

Next morning, the storm had passed. The wind had died down and the storm clouds had gone from the sky. Bright sunshine streamed in through the Palace windows, and it was a beautiful day.

The Princess, however, came in to breakfast looking very pale and tired.

"Did you sleep well?" the Queen asked her.

"No, indeed I did not," she replied with a yawn. "In fact, I couldn't sleep a wink." And the poor Princess rubbed her back. "I think I must have been lying on a rock, the bed felt so hard and uncomfortable."

The Prince looked at the King in dismay —
but the Queen told them not to worry. How she
laughed as she led the Princess back to her bedroom.

One by one the pageboys took away the
feather quilts. Then one by one the maids took away
the mattresses. And there, lying right in the middle of
the bed, was one tiny dried PEA!

"Only a real, genuine Princess could feel a
tiny dried pea through all those quilts and
mattresses," laughed the Queen with delight.

When the Prince heard the story he asked the Princess to marry him. Not because she had proved she was a real, genuine Princess — but because he had fallen in love with her when he first saw her.

So, the Prince married the Princess and they were very happy together.

They kept the tiny dried pea on a velvet cushion inside a special glass case. This would keep it quite safe. In the years to come their children could take a look at it — and in many years, perhaps their grandchildren too!

# HANSEL AND GRETEL

Once upon a time, there lived on the edge of a dark forest, a poor woodcutter, his wife and two children. The little boy was called Hansel and the little girl's name was Gretel.

When the children were small, the woodcutter had lots of work and everyone had plenty to eat. But sad to say, their happiness did not last. The woodcutter's wife died, and the poor man chose another, who turned out to be cruel and selfish.

One day a great famine came to the land, leaving everyone short of food. The poor woodcutter was very worried as they had only one piece of bread left. His family would soon starve.

Hansel and Gretel's cruel stepmother made sure that she wouldn't starve. ''Tomorrow morning, take the children to the thickest part of the forest, and leave them,'' she said. ''Someone may come along and take pity on them and perhaps give them some food. For if they stay with us they will starve anyway.''

She pleaded and argued so much that the woodcutter was forced to agree with her evil suggestion. Hansel and Gretel had not been able to sleep, because they were so hungry. And they heard every word their parents had said.

''Don't cry, Gretel,'' said the boy to his little sister, ''for I have thought of a plan to find our way home again.''

The moon was shining brightly as Hansel
climbed out of his bedroom window and jumped
down onto the path. He filled both his pockets with
small white pebbles, then crept quietly back to bed.

Early next morning, the poor woodcutter led
his children deeper and deeper into the forest.

Clever Hansel trailed behind, pretending to be
watching the birds. Every so often he let fall a shiny
white pebble from his pocket.

When it grew dark, the woodcutter built a
huge fire. His children were so tired that they fell
asleep in front of it. When they woke up, their father
had gone.

Little Gretel was very frightened, and began to cry. "Don't worry," Hansel told his sister. "Wait until the moon comes out."

Once the moon had risen, the children could see the pebbles shining brightly on the forest path. They followed them, and by morning they were home.

Their father was overjoyed to see his dear children again, but their cruel stepmother was very angry because the plan had failed.

It wasn't long before she began to argue and plead with the woodcutter once more. "There is not enough food left to feed us all," she screamed. "Get rid of your children, or we shall all die."

This time (to make sure the woodcutter made no more mistakes), the stepmother went along to see that Hansel and Gretel were left to die in the forest.

However, she did not notice Hansel throwing down tiny crumbs of bread onto the forest path.

Once again, the woodcutter made the children a roaring fire, and once again they both fell fast asleep.

When the children woke up and found themselves alone, they began to search for the breadcrumbs. But, alas, the birds had eaten them all up. Poor Hansel and Gretel, they sat down and cried themselves to sleep by the fire.

In the morning, when it grew light, the two set
off to find their way home. In fact, they were just walking
round in circles — deeper and deeper into the forest.

It was then that Hansel noticed a tiny white
bird sitting on a branch. The bird began to sing,
"Follow me, follow me." It flew in front of the
children until it reached a little house in a clearing.

It was the most unusual house you could
dream of. The walls were made of gingerbread and
the roof of cake and biscuits. The windows were sugar
and the doors were peppermint sticks. Hansel and
Gretel were so hungry that they began to eat bits and
pieces off the house.

Then the door opened and an old woman hobbled out. At first the children drew back in fear. "Come inside, my dears," she smiled, "and I will look after you."

The old woman cooked them a lovely dinner and showed them two little beds, covered with soft pillows and blankets. That night the children fell asleep thinking they were safe and sound at last.

Poor Hansel and Gretel. They had fallen right into a trap. The old woman was really an evil witch, whose favourite food was children!

Very early next morning, the witch grabbed the sleeping Hansel and locked him in a cage.

Next, she shook Gretel hard. "Wake up girl and cook your brother a huge breakfast. When he is fat enough I shall eat him."

Day after day, Gretel had to cook huge meals to fatten-up her brother.

Now, the witch was very short-sighted. Every morning she would make Hansel stick his finger out of the cage — just to see how much he had grown. But the boy was crafty. Instead of his finger, he would poke a chicken bone through the bars. "You're still too thin," she would scream, and make Gretel cook even more food.

Week after week went by, until the witch could wait no longer. "I shall eat him right away!" she cackled.

Without wasting a moment, the old witch dragged Gretel into the kitchen. She made the terrified girl stoke the fire until the oven was red hot. ''Is the oven ready for roasting?'' called the witch with glee.

''I cannot tell,'' answered Gretel, pretending not to understand.

This made the witch very angry. ''Stupid girl,'' she cried, as she pulled Gretel across the room. ''This is how it's done,'' and the witch bent over and stuck her head in the oven.

Gretel gave her one great push, and the evil witch fell inside and was burnt to a crisp.

Swiftly, Gretel freed her brother from that awful cage, and the children danced for joy.

Before they left for home, they found a pile of gold hidden in the witch's cottage.

Then, as if by magic, a new path opened up through the forest. It led to a broad river where a great white duck was waiting to take them across.

Very soon they saw their own dear house through the trees. Their wicked stepmother had died, and their father was a sad and sorry man.

Luckily, Hansel and Gretel soon forgot about the wicked witch. They forgave their poor father and all lived happily ever after.

# THE PIED PIPER OF HAMELIN

Long, long ago in Hamelin Town, Germany, something happened almost too strange to tell. Nevertheless, this story has been passed down through generations of parents to their children — until it has become a legend.

The town of Hamelin lay on the banks of the River Weser. It was a very pleasant place to live. The people of the town were prosperous and had more than enough to eat. Their pantries and larders were piled high with rich tasty food, and their cellars were packed with the best wines. They wore the finest clothes of velvet trimmed with fur, and shoes of the softest leather.

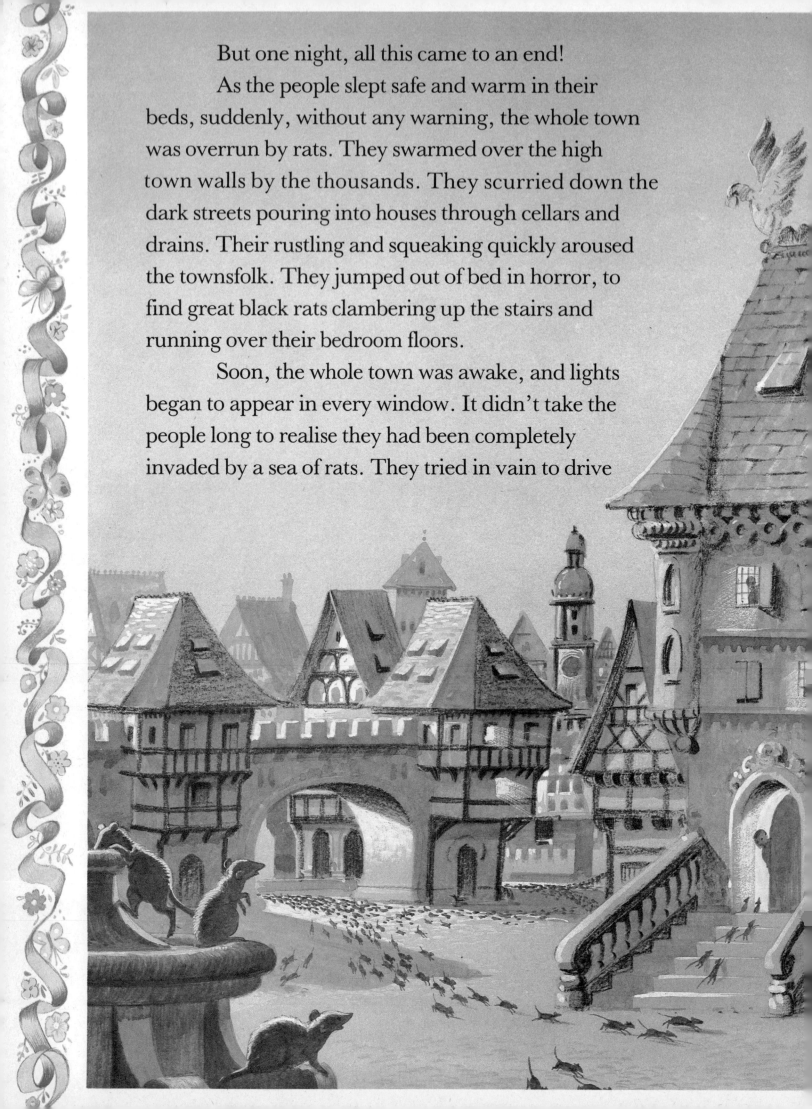

But one night, all this came to an end!

As the people slept safe and warm in their beds, suddenly, without any warning, the whole town was overrun by rats. They swarmed over the high town walls by the thousands. They scurried down the dark streets pouring into houses through cellars and drains. Their rustling and squeaking quickly aroused the townsfolk. They jumped out of bed in horror, to find great black rats clambering up the stairs and running over their bedroom floors.

Soon, the whole town was awake, and lights began to appear in every window. It didn't take the people long to realise they had been completely invaded by a sea of rats. They tried in vain to drive them out of their houses, chasing them out with sticks and pokers, in fact, anything they could lay their hands on. But it was no good!

To make matters worse, the plague of rats began to eat everything in sight. They gobbled all the food from the tables. They ran across the kitchen stoves and ate the stew and soup straight from the bubbling pans. There were rats in the flour sacks, rats in the milk churns, and every scrap of butter and cheese vanished in a trice. They even stole the loaves of hot bread baking in the ovens! It wasn't long before every scrap of food in the town had disappeared, eaten by the rats. The shops were all empty, even the taverns had no food or drink left.

Everyone began to feel hungry for the first time, and they were worried that they might soon starve. Something must be done! The people of Hamelin were desperate. Groups of them gathered on street corners muttering and complaining. Then they started to march through the town, joining together until they formed a great crowd outside the Town Hall, where everyone began to shout for the Mayor.

The crowd sounded so angry that the Mayor's knees knocked together with fright. He had been locked in his chamber with all the town councillors for days. Not one of them could think of a solution.

All at once the crowd grew quiet. A stranger appeared from nowhere, stepped up to the Town Hall, knocked on the Mayor's door and went inside!

He was the strangest figure — his queer long coat, from heel to head, was half of yellow and half of red. He himself was tall and thin, with sharp blue eyes, each like a pin.

The stranger spoke up, "If I rid your town of rats, will you give me a thousand gilders?"

The Mayor stared in astonishment, "I will give you not one thousand gilders, but fifty thousand!"

Around the stranger's neck hung a pipe. "People call me the Pied Piper," he said, and without another word he stepped into the street and started to play. He had only uttered three notes, when the rats began to appear. They poured out of the houses and into the streets in their thousands, following the music as if they were bewitched. Through the streets the Piper led the rats, out of the town gates, until he came to the banks of the River Weser.

There the Pied Piper stopped his playing, and as if with one accord, the rats jumped into the river and were drowned! A mighty cheer went up from all the townsfolk watching from the walls. How they cheered the Pied Piper as he hurried back to collect his reward from the Mayor.

As he reached the Town Hall the Mayor shouted from the steps, ''Be off with you, Piper! I owe you nothing for just playing one tune.'' Then the Mayor laughed in the Piper's face. ''The rats are gone and can't come back, go blow your pipe 'til you burst!''

Once more the Piper stepped into the street. He put his pipe to his lips again and began to blow. The notes he played were so sweet that all the crowds in the street stopped, spellbound by the music.

Then, there came such a rustling and a bustling. Small feet were pattering, wooden shoes clattering, little hands clapping and little tongues chattering. Out came the children running, all the little boys and girls with rosy cheeks and flaxen curls were tripping and skipping, running merrily after that wonderful music with shouts and laughter.

The Mayor, the council and the parents stood, as if they were changed into blocks of wood — unable to move a step or cry out, as the children merrily skipped by. The Piper led them through the gates of the town. On and on they danced, over fields, down lanes, until they were far into the countryside. How the townsfolk cried and called after their children, but they didn't seem to hear.

Suddenly, the Piper turned his steps towards the mountains, the townspeople's cries turned to joy. ''He can't cross that mountain top,'' the Mayor sighed with relief. ''He must let his piping drop, and then our children will stop.''

As the children reached the mountain side, a great door opened wide. The Piper went in and the children followed. And when they were all safe inside — the door in the mountain shut fast.

All except one little boy, as he was lame, he couldn't dance the whole of the way. Unable to keep up with the others, he had been left behind.

The Mayor of Hamelin searched far and wide for the Pied Piper, offering all the gold and silver in the town, if only the Piper could bring the children back. But Piper and children were gone forever.

The legend says they went to a better land where people always keep their promises — especially to Pipers!